ASH ABOVE, SNOW BELOW

FREDRICK NILES

FEVER GARDEN PUBLISHING

ASH ABOVE, SNOW BELOW

First edition. December 9, 2018.

ISBN: 978-1-950021-01-7

Fever Garden Publishing

Cover art by: artonthedl.com

❀ Created with Vellum

Dedicated to my dad.

"That which is below is like that which is above & that which is above is like that which is below to do the miracles of one only thing"
   -from Isaac Newton's translation of The Emerald Tablet

"For what happens to the children of man and what happens to the beasts is the same; as one dies, so dies the other. They all have the same breath, and man has no advantage over the beasts, for all is vanity. All go to one place. All are from the dust, and to dust all return. Who knows whether the spirit of man goes upward and the spirit of the beast goes down into the earth? So I saw that there is nothing better than that a man should rejoice in his work, for that is his lot. Who can bring him to see what will be after him?"
   -Ecclesiastes 3:19-22 (ESV)

"As above, so below
   Dismantled piece by piece
   What's left will not decease
   As within, so without
   The seasons bring relief
   Let me live and die in peace"
   -Memento Mori, Architects

1

JOSHUA

The small house was one of the coldest places Joshua had ever been. It was a tiny cluster of boards and nails that rattled and creaked relentlessly as an easterly wind attempted to tear it up by the roots and hurl it into the mountain range that jutted up along the horizon. If the living room had been any sparer, it would have been a hole in the ground. No table, no real furniture. Nothing but a single rocking chair that had sat facing out the window until Joshua swung it towards the door.

Now, rocking gently back and forth, Joshua felt the cool grip of the matte-black Sig Sauer he had found tucked away in an old bunker just two months before. Finding something so pristine—so *unblemished*—made the gun feel almost like a gift. He hadn't believed his eyes when he had dug the dusty case out of its little hiding place underneath the empty food crate. He had found it quite by accident, really. The small room had been ransacked of food and other supplies long ago, but in a desperate attempt to search the small venting duct cut four inches from the ceiling along the back wall, he had tried to climb one of the metal shelves that had once held countless boxes and cans of non-perishables, but had since become a bare skeleton of weak metal. Relieved of its contents, the shelf had begun to tip after Joshua—placing both feet on the bottom shelf—tried to use it as a ladder. And once it began to topple, there was no stopping it. Joshua leaped backward as the large, metal frame began to descend upon him, and he just barely managed to drop to the ground and roll out of the way before it came crashing onto the cement floor with a sound so loud he could have sworn the very earth itself had split open.

Supplies were scarce in The Valley, so it was second nature for Joshua to check under and behind where the shelf had been. He didn't think he was likely to find anything, but he couldn't afford to miss something if it was there. Even so, he may still have missed it if it hadn't been for the bright light that had shone down from the entryway and illuminated a dip in the concrete that, upon further inspection was revealed to be not concrete at all, but a perfectly square hole in the ground that had been covered with a grey towel and packed with dirt. Dirt, and a compact, airtight case.

After opening the case, Joshua stared for a long time. Inside lay two loaded magazines and a smooth, black automatic pistol. He could hardly believe his eyes. Most of the weapons wielded around here were blunt instruments, barbed harpoons, rusty knives, or—if one were extremely lucky—a worn, old rifle or revolver with less than five shots in it.

Ammunition was practically nowhere to be found in these parts, but even so, Joshua's empty stomach had eventually torn him from his reverie and prompted him to climb back up the ladder to the bunker and out into the cold, whereupon he shot and ate the first living thing he had come across: one of the large scavenging birds that were never far from anything that still drew breath.

Joshua remembered how the plucked animal, already becoming stiff with rigor mortis, had popped and spat over the little fire, and how his body screamed with hunger until he could take it no longer, and finally picked up the carcass and devoured anything and everything that could fit down his throat without getting caught. He remembered how it had been slightly cooked on the outside, but still raw and gummy in the middle. It didn't matter.

Since then, he hadn't fired another shot.

The mere sight of a firearm around here was an experience that verged on being holy. A steel black deity unto which one knelt or was made to kneel, to come crashing to the earth like some scorned devil by the flashing thunderbolts that issued forth from the shrunken eye of the barrel, a pupil that issued light rather than receive it—that winked with the striking of an internal hammer.

And now he held this little god in his hand. He held purpose in his heart. And judgment in his eyes.

Joshua had been sitting for about five hours now. The person who lived here was sure to be returning soon, and the wind was so loud outside that he had no illusions about being able to hear his approach. Even so, he felt his body involuntarily tense in the seconds before the front door began to rattle on its hinges.

After what seemed to be a struggle with the handle, it finally slammed open to reveal a withered, old man who shook and clamored at the door as he tried to push it shut and replace the inner latch.

"Sorry," the old man gasped apologetically as he hobbled inside. He had a worn walking stick in one hand and was dressed in grey and matted rags. "Getting up that hill with this old body is like trying to climb a ladder with your teeth."

Joshua remained silent. He had of course been expected. In the snow, there was only so much you could do to hide your tracks. He had circled around the back of the house, all the while steering clear of the main trail. A tiny window with a board nailed over it was easy enough to pry open and climb through. But he had known that the old man—no matter how resigned—would still observe and move through the world in the same way he always had: carefully.

"That's the way of it though, isn't it?" The man gestured at the chair with his free hand and Joshua got up and moved aside so he could sit down. "The way forward is always easier than the way back."

"I've found the opposite to be true," Joshua said.

"Well," the old man hesitated as if he were searching for something. "I suppose that means you're chasing the wrong the thing. All anyone wants to do is go back. Back to happiness, back to innocence. So it would stand to reason that every step forward is a step in the wrong direction then, right?"

"That's actually why I'm here," Joshua said, trying to shift the conversation. "There's a rumor going around that you know."

"Know what?"

"The way back." Joshua towered over the hunched figure. "The way *out*."

The man gave a nod as his fingers unconsciously fidgeted with the hem of his shirt.

"Did you find them?" The words were quiet, almost a whisper.

"I did," Joshua said.

The small hole in the ground had gaped up at him like a foul mouth, lined with teeth made of small and dirty bones placed inexpertly in every direction. It was impossible to tell how long they had been there, but if Joshua's information was correct it had been many years. Many years of patiently laying and waiting to be exhumed. Though no flesh would ever cling to them again, their confirmed existence would raise them from the dead and bare their vengeance as an eternal plague that passed from person to person and crushed those in its wake.

A young woman and two pre-adolescent girls. They hadn't been Joshua's, but he was determined to deliver their justice all the same. The hole they had been dumped in was deeper than it was wide, so their bodies had to be stacked on top of one another as their skulls, necks, and faces were caved in by the large stones that had been fastened to pieces of wood for this singular purpose.

"Tell me," Joshua said, "Is it the peak?"

"The God's Eye?" The words came out like a curse.

For the first time the old man stared up and into Joshua's eyes, and for a brief moment, he thought that the door had blown back open and filled the room with icy wind.

"That is not the way out. That is not the way anywhere. There are men who have walked that trail. The steep and treacherous path that leads only to the top offers escape but delivers only madness. The view offers clarity, that much is true. It offers it in the same way a mortal man sees a cloud of smoke. The particles are only visible in their multitude, but it is their very number that obscures everything else. Mark my words son, if you climb that mountain and look out over The Valley, you will cast yourself right off of it."

"Then what?" Joshua hissed in sudden fury. "How? And if you have found it—found the way out—then why haven't *you* left?"

"Who says I haven't?" And with those words, the man sounded not like a man, but like a child. Like a small boy asking what the moon is made of or how many stars there are.

"You can still get out of this alive," Joshua said.

The man's eyes brightened, making him look even younger. "Who says that's not what I want?"

The blow landed on the left side of the man's jaw, and the added weight of the handgun sent him sprawling out of the chair and onto the floor. He spat out more than a few teeth.

Joshua clicked the safety off and pointed the barrel at the man. Suddenly looking far more elderly, he rolled over, reached up, and gingerly touched the side of his face that was now broken open and bleeding. He rubbed the blood between his fingers without looking at it and then turned his head so the wound was pressed against his left shoulder.

"Last chance," Joshua said. "One more riddle and I'll shoot you right through the chest. How do I get out of this shit-hole?"

"How'd you get here?" His voice had turned into a wheeze.

"The river."

"Remember what I said about going back the way you came?"

Joshua ran a shaking hand through his hair. He looked around the room. Boards rotted and twisted with age clung to each other and huddled around nothing but a chair and a crumpled and soiled comforter in the corner. No food. No supplies. "It seems to me that you're a man with one foot in the grave."

"True enough," the man laughed. "But am I stepping in or stepping out?"

"In, I'd say." The gun bucked in Joshua's hand as it clapped and punched a tunnel through the old man's chest. He didn't fly back or gasp out in shock. He simply kept breathing, but now there was a high pitched whistling sound that went up and down with his labored breaths.

Finally, after what seemed like an age but what was probably closer to a few seconds, the man slumped and his eyelids half-slid over his already vacant stare.

Joshua clicked the safety back on, tucked the gun back into his belt, and quietly turned around to let himself out the front door by which he had not entered.

For hours afterward, the wind blew through the trees and the branches vibrated and whistled like the old man's chest had, not like a signal of danger, but like a train, as it left an empty station, bearing its passenger back home.

2

JOSHUA

Another silver dusk had arrived and once again Joshua was stuck under a tree, burrowed into the snow. He huddled like a fallen fruit from times past. A dead seed in the shadowed valley. The earth, if you could call it that, was white. For all he knew, it was frozen right down to its core. Nights were always the worst. Accusations sang through the wind and swung through the branches. Trees croaked and muttered when he passed by. Animals stared with knowing eyes.

They called it The Valley, but the indentation of land in which Joshua now found himself was more like the corner of a boxing ring. Steep and jagged mountains towered up from the North and East, an endless and uncrossable tundra stretched to the West, and to the South lay the ocean. Deep and formless, a great body of water that hurled storm after storm against the land.

Joshua once spoke with a woman who had tried to cross it with her son and daughter, but within hours the waves had swallowed all three and spat her back up on shore. She had said it felt like a miracle at first—the fact that she hadn't died from hypothermia alone defied all logic. But when she had searched for her children, she realized that it wasn't a guardian angel that hovered over her, but a curse, deceiving and mocking. Her loneliness a new and terrible verse in the sad song of her life.

The tundra was a different breed of terrible. Flat and barren, the winds could reach speeds that could tear skin and muscle from bone. In fact, it almost seemed to defy some law of nature. The winds on the water were bad but they were worse on the tundra somehow. More Savage. They almost seemed to be driven by some sort of consciousness—some intentional malice.

Joshua had tried to cross it twice: once with a caravan and once by himself.

When he had gone by himself, he had been literally blown off of his feet and dropped back onto the ground like a child's plaything. He didn't make it two miles before turning back.

The caravan had consisted of four wagons, twelve people, and eighteen slaves. He remembered how the wind had picked up the skinny wretches attached to the reigns and whisked them away like autumn leaves. Seeing grown men hurled around by nothing but air had reduced four of the people to quivering wrecks and the few slaves that had survived by crouching behind the wagons refused to move until one of them was killed by one of the masters as an example.

Joshua liked neither slavery nor slaves.

Men and women were abducted from their homes, packed together in stables and basements, made to crawl in the dirt and slush and eventually, they became something else. Some resigned and defeated, others angry and treacherous. Joshua didn't like them because they needed feeding and mending. They existed for no other purpose but to allow their masters to be lazy. And oftentimes they would fall in and literally devour their owners. That, or they would all kill each other but for a few, and when only three or four were left, they would make the master the slave. They would make him find the food, build the shelters, scrape the shit off of the floor. And soon after that they would grow bored with their vengeance and kill him, go separate ways, and maybe sometime in the future would become masters themselves. But more likely, slaves again.

Slavery was the law of the land in The Valley. If you weren't a slave to a person, then you were a slave to hunger or hatred or exhaustion.

When the slave crouched behind the wagon-wheel had refused to move, Joshua watched one of the large and hairy men that were giving the orders pull a hammer from his belt and slam it into the back of the slave's head. He had then pointed it at Joshua, who was also crouched behind the wagon and ordered him to get behind and push. Just like that, Joshua had been enslaved, for here, the master was the stone, the knife, the gun. The master was brute strength and willpower, and at that moment, Joshua had been assessed and deemed weaker than the man with the hammer. And that may have been true in a literal sense. Joshua probably *was* weaker, but after the man had turned around to yell at the others Joshua had slid up behind him and opened his throat with the jagged hunk of steel he kept in his boot. He stabbed him once, twice, could have been a thousand times. He wasn't counting. He just did his work without emotion, and he didn't stop until the screams did.

The wind howled on for hours and by the time it was finished both master and slave had been depleted in number to the point where only five remained. Some had been picked up and hurled in great gusts. Some shredded by one of the wagons after it had come apart. Some murdered each other. Some of them had just flat-out lost their minds. But when the few remained, it was clear that there was only one master: the land.

The survivors fled back the way they had come once the wind let up, and whether they had embarked pulling a wagon or in the back of one, they all returned on shaking knees, and departed from each other as soon as they got the chance.

Joshua hadn't stepped foot onto the tundra since, nor had he even so much as considered traveling with a caravan. Except for a small harbor town to the South that served more as a rest-stop than an actual place of residence, people around here were almost *always* worse in numbers.

Tonight, Joshua felt notably colder. In his leather boots and fur jacket, he shifted and hugged himself for warmth. He had spent so much time searching. So much time wasted chasing down that old bag of bones just to be told to go back up the river. Fuck him. He knew what that meant. That old bastard knew he was going to die and probably thought he might as well damn his murderer too. Still. It was a way. If only the damn river would freeze. But no, for that giant, churning thing to freeze solid it would have to drop to a hundred below zero. He would have walked along the shore if there had been one, but centuries of the water's steady sawing had carved right through the rock and all that stood on either side were cliffs.

Something croaked dryly in the distance and Joshua pulled his legs up closer. He had a large blanket wrapped around him and was under at least two feet of snow. Despite all that, however, he knew there were still things that could find him. Track him.

Joshua tried not to move but every so often he would begin to shiver for a minute, then stop. He had to stop thinking about how he was going to get out. At least for tonight. Tomorrow he would decide if he would brave the river or not.

Right now he had to sleep.

THE NEXT MORNING wasn't as much a morning as it was another stage of night. Slightly brighter, yes, but with the same kind of hushed fear that came out when the owls did.

Under a ceiling of bushy, grey clouds there circled a bird. Featherless and extraordinarily broad, it moved like a dark storm cloud over the raw landscape. Beneath it, down where the food darted in and out of their holes, it spied a moving black dot. Moving black dots often meant a meal. All-day long animals would zig-zag dotted paths over the paper-white snow, and when two of those lines met at exactly the same time, usually only one of them would continue on. This dot, however, moved slower and more deliberately than most. Its steady plotting was less like a stalking wolf or wandering deer, and more like that of the moon across the sky on a long night. The bird decided that an oddity as such certainly warranted a closer look.

It didn't land on the tree branch as much as struck it like a black arrow. Snow and bits of bark exploded off of the limb and startled Joshua so severely that he almost fell backward into the snow.

"What you want, demon?" he spat angrily.

The bird hunched and stared like a great winged spider and clacked its beak. The creature was easily as tall as Joshua and if it were to unfold its charred, rib-like wings, it would have equaled the length of a pick-up truck.

Pick-up truck, thought Joshua. A memory from another age flashed by him. He shuddered.

The bird opened its cavernous mouth, as if to eat the sprouting nightmare in Joshua's head. It stretched its long neck forward and snapped its beak with a loud clap.

Joshua's nightmare slithered back into the dark.

After a brief stare-off, it became clear that the bird wasn't going anywhere. Joshua thought about shooting it, but he didn't want to waste the ammunition. Not to mention the fact that when a shot was fired down in The Valley, it couldn't be guaranteed that something else wouldn't come running. He shouldn't have shot the crow that time, but he had been hungry to the point of near blindness. He shouldn't have even shot the old man—should have just caved his head in like he had done to so many others—but walking through the wilderness with a gun in your belt and murder in your heart, with hours and hours to dwell on it, would always paint images in your mind that, given the chance, would almost always render themselves physically.

Joshua reached down, scooped up a handful of snow, and after packing it into a tight ball, hurled it at the creature. He missed.

Fine. To hell with the thing. But when he started moving forward, the bird hopped to the next branch. After another fifteen feet, the bird jumped again to a tree out in front of him. It was following him and it didn't take a genius to guess that a following scavenger meant dark times ahead.

THE BODIES WERE LYING in a heap inside a patch of melted snow, or at least, what once had been bodies. Now they were one body. A twisted and gnarled conglomeration of charred flesh and jutting bone. All had been burned away. Skin, hair, lips, toenails. All had been scorched and melted. Even the shackles that must have been attached to the slaves were blackened and broken in a crude mockery of freedom. All was destroyed.

Everything but the eyes.

It was what had first caught his attention. Not the smell of flesh nor the sight of so much black in a world of snow. It was the feeling of being watched. Something that involves a person's sight taking in every single detail as they look around. Leaves, branches, twigs, dirt, rocks. It takes it in all at once and translates it. Forest, ridge, field. And somewhere in there, even from a long way off, that sight had seen the bright sheen of a human eyeball. It was too distant for the conscious brain to acknowledge, too small a spark in a tidal wave of information. But deep in the subconscious, a red light glowed in warning. *You are being watched.*

Now the melted mass of former men and women lay staring in every direction. And there was something about the eyes, about the color and wetness, that made them look as if they did not belong to the dead, or at the very least, did not belong to a body that had ceased to observe.

Joshua reached down and gripped the gun for assurance. As he walked away, he had the distinct feeling, that the eyes were following him.

3

JOSHUA

The sun was hardly visible. It moved elusively across the sky and the clouds overhead blocked more than their fair share of light, casting the earth in a sort of perpetual dusk. As it made its journey around, Joshua had been steadily increasing his speed. He pushed over the land like a storm front. Animals felt his presence and altered their activities. Movement began to lessen in the brush. Holes and nooks became occupied. A change was on its way and small souls took notice.

The river. He had to reach the river. And from there? He'd worry about that then.

The fields that stretched out around him were vast and snow-scorched. Up ahead, a scattering of dark deciduous trees punctured their way up through the ground to sway in the wind and their constant motion reminded Joshua of a giant, gnashing maw. A maw that he knew, over time, would eventually ground him down into the ashy snow he currently tread upon.

If the vulture was looking down on him now—and it very well could be, he had lost track of it a few hours ago—it would no longer see a slow-moving walker, but something more like a frantic sprinter.

The snow was getting deeper. The trees around him were

becoming thicker. Small branches full of what felt like tiny slivers of ice slapped him in the face as he ran, but he still hurdled forward in a typhoon of noise and motion.

IT WAS NEARING dark when he finally saw one. He had felt their presence all day. Felt eyes upon him when he stopped to eat from a can of green beans he had traded for a few weeks ago. Felt the silence of the animals slowly squeezing around him like a giant hand. Somewhere out there, there was something following him. Maybe many things. He couldn't tell. He couldn't see it. Couldn't hear it.

He could smell it.

It was like decay mixed with the odor of some poisonous, underground gas. Rotting meat and wet dog.

The muscles in his legs burned. His knees felt like they had melted and they sloshed back and forth as he struggled forward. In addition to his failing body, the snow was becoming thicker and deeper.

One more step.

Then without warning, solid ground vanished out from under him. Joshua found himself thrashing in thick, wet snow up to his neck. Shit. He wished he had grabbed one of the tiny collapsible shovels he had seen being sold for small fortunes at the mobile market. Those were for home-folk though. Non-nomads they called themselves. Built homes up in the Northern foothills. Joshua had always just called them future slaves.

And slaves they might be, he thought to himself. But at least they weren't stuck in a fucking thousand feet of densely packed snow. He pushed a few feet forward and found that if he lifted and kicked his feet, he could make progress.

Feeling pretty good about himself after a few minutes, Joshua's confidence was instantly extinguished. He had seen it. *Could* see it, if he focused at just the right angle. A giant black shape slunk back and forth in a clump of trees to his left. It moved through them like water and over the snow like smoke. It wasn't moving in his direction, but he wasn't stupid.

He was being circled.

There was a brief moment of silence that followed. In it, he could hear the whoosh of water from somewhere nearby and it occurred to him that the sound had been steadily increasing over the last half-hour, but he had failed to acknowledge it in his charge through the deep snow.

Joshua exploded forward. He moved so furiously that he began to gain purchase on the snow underneath him and could run without having his feet plunge all the way to the bottom. It was difficult and still painfully slow, but fear surged through him like a current and powered him towards a large stretch of hardwoods that lay before him.

He could feel them. He kept catching movement out of the corner of his eyes. They were tightening the noose. The next time he looked up from his thrashing he saw that he had breached the edge of the woods and was now moving through the heavy timber. Maybe he could climb one of the trees. The snow was still up to his chest, so perhaps, if he moved gently enough, he could stand on top of it without breaking the thin, icy crust and reach one of the lower branches. He reached down and felt the gun in his belt. His pursuers might be able to climb, but he had yet to run into anything that could dodge bullets. Still, it was now so dark that it'd be hard to see what he was shooting at until it was right on top of him.

One of the trees towered over him and dangled a branch just mockingly out of reach. But if he could just find purchase on the top of the snow...

THE CREATURE MOVED in a long and loping gait. Its wide paws landed in the snow and pushed off in rapid succession without breaking the surface. Deceptively light, the beast could have moved in whenever it wanted, the webbing between its toes acting like snowshoes to distribute its weight. But it wanted its prey to feel the fear. Wanted it to know it was being hunted.

Night had fully descended and the tall timbers stretched up like the hand of some great submerged beast. The man they were hunting, the one that had spilled blood in the little house and ignited every feral instinct to track and stalk and kill, had disappeared behind one of the trees. A deep howl broke the night air, rose in pitch, and flattened out on a note of fevered hunger. The time to move was now.

The dark shadows closed on the tree like a snare, but when they reached it, they realized the man was no longer on the ground. The smell was intoxicating. Sour and ripe at the same time, the fear and hatred hung in the air as if on a meat hook.

Claws scarred the tree's bark and burned the wood underneath, causing wisps of smoke to rise and dissipate. They knew he was armed. They expected a fight, but he was not firing. Not screaming. Not making a noise. The creature, with its hind legs on the snow and front legs pressed against the tree, stopped and sniffed the air. It lowered itself to all fours and looked down. Saw how the snow had caved in at certain points, and then some short distance away it saw a hole had appeared and the trail of the man resumed. And there he was.

TUNNELING HAD FELT like a good idea at first. If he had gone up that tree it would have all been over. But as soon as he started scooping handfuls of snow away and pushing it behind him, he realized just how claustrophobic the space around him was. The snow wasn't nearly as deep now, and he had to crawl on his belly to stay submerged. He felt something pass by him and froze. It wasn't the thumping of feet or the disturbance in the snow, it was more like a chill. A feeling. Joshua knew that if they stepped on the thin layer of snow above the tunnel he had dug, they would fall through and it would all be over. He lay like a corpse in a grave.

He counted to three.

One. Two. He gripped the handle of the pistol. *Three...*

He pushed his feet up and sprang forward. Quickly but quietly. The snow dampened the sound of movement and he could hear the furious scratching of claws on tree bark. He couldn't help it. He turned around to look.

It was like a dog. A wolf, but not precisely. It stood hunched and sniffing, flaring its wide nostrils above the snow. It saw the trail. Saw that it had miraculously passed by its prey. And with that, it looked up and straight into Joshua's eyes.

And it saw everything.

THE CREATURE WAS EASILY TWICE the size of a normal wolf and Joshua watched the hackles on the back of its neck rise and bristle. He watched the other heads turn towards him. Watched the one nearest him fix him with its dull, amber glowing eyes that were set in its cavernous skull like two agates.

Then he watched it slowly stand upright on two powerful back legs.

4

SIMONE

Simone hadn't *not* pissed herself in three days. The getting up, the unbuckling, the squatting in the snow; it was all just way too much movement. She had picked this spot on purpose. It was right underneath a low cliff that jutted out and hid her from anyone descending from above. Similarly, the rocks below and to her left were too steep for anyone to climb without significant commotion. The only way up was the way she had taken: right in front of her. It was a small goat path etched into the side of the cliff. Having neither an accommodating incline nor any real destination but the wall of rock she was nestled against, it saw very little traffic. Perhaps they had once patrolled it like they had the perimeters of the other camps: frequently and with dogs. But if it were like all the other camps then their patrol numbers had thinned, their discipline gone slack.

And their stomachs grown hungry.

Dogs were seldom seen in The Valley any more. Occasionally there would be the rare K-9 that possessed acute senses and a superior sense of caution, but more often than not a dog in The Valley was just another doomed animal on the lonely, frozen carapace of the world. Stricken by famine. Hunted by the famished.

Now the hills and cliffs remained unobserved but for a few wasted goat herds. More than a few times in the last couple days Simone had watched one of the gaunt and haunted animals jump from one precarious ledge to another, only to have the wind-rattled rocks give way and release another soul to the void.

A loud chorus of laughter erupted from down below. Laughter was rare in Simone's experience, and cheer was extinct. So she felt little surprise when she discovered the source of their amusement.

One of the slaves had tried to kill himself. Young. Mid-twenties probably. Prime age for labor. He had tried to hang himself with the very rope that bound him. Everyone knew that the sleeping houses were short enough to climb but tall enough to allow someone to jump out of the cage. They also knew that the rope attached to the slaves' steel collars were nowhere near long enough to see them to the ground. The young man almost certainly knew all of this but had jumped anyway. He had sought escape, to be sure, but only the escape offered by the pale hands of death.

He hadn't succeeded though. The rope was too elastic to break his neck, so now he just hung thrashing against the outside of the cage. Maybe he would have died in minutes. Maybe even less if he had managed to cut off the circulation to his brain. But as soon as he had jumped over the side, the guards came running. Technically, their job was to save him. He was a valuable piece of property, and it was their job to make sure nothing happened to him. But long, boring days can bring out more savagery in people than short, brutal ones.

Five figures huddled around the choking man, and whenever his movement would begin to slow or his face would begin to turn purple, one of them would grab his legs, hoist him back up, and let him gasp lungfuls of air for a few seconds. Then they would gently lower him back down.

Most of the slaves here were kept in a large cage in the middle of the camp. Food was thrown down from a walkway that stretched out overhead, and water was poured into a trough that ran lengthwise along the Southside of the enclosure. Most of the time they just stood still, huddled together for warmth, which as it turned out, was surprisingly effective with people of such a large number. The more valuable slaves, however, got their own pens that lined the West edge of the camps. Each pen contained a small 6X6 shed in which each person could sleep.

And they were people. Simone had never doubted that.

The prevailing idea was that once someone had become a slave, they either surrendered their personhood or their lives. After all, if you didn't value your freedom enough to die for it, then you didn't desire it at all. She had tried to explain it to someone once—tried to explain to him that you had a choice: freedom or slavery. It was as simple as that. Death never factored into it, because in the end, what was slavery but death incarnate. If you wanted to be free, you would choose freedom. If you wanted to be a slave, you would be a slave.

But she thought differently now. She knew better because she had been at the brink. She had been about to go down with flesh beneath her nails and blood staining her teeth. But it hadn't just been her. It wasn't just her life at stake. To this day she wondered if she had chosen correctly.

The dying boy was almost there. His body radiated exhaustion. His gaze had become more and more vacant with every passing second. Soon his heart would give out.

Simone slowly lowered her cheek against the rifle stock that had been pressed against her shoulder for the last 70 hours. The biggest guard's face was blotted out with the middle peg of the iron sight and then came back into view as she accounted for wind speed and bullet drop.

"Pow," she whispered.

She sighted the next guard and the next. Four men and a woman now that she was focusing on their faces. All of them should be dropping. Her heart burned with such a cold and throbbing hatred that if it had been made manifest, the world itself would have been squeezed in her grip until it popped like the head of some small and feral monster. She wanted to shoot the rope from which the man hung. But she didn't. 200 yards. She was that good once. Maybe still was, but she wasn't sure. She could even just shoot the boy. End his torment and rob his tormentors.

But she didn't.

Three shots. That's all she had left after her last kill. One .308 round lay in the chamber of her weapon like some messiah yet to rise. The other two were packed snuggly in her pack along with a blanket, a gun cleaning kit, and a change of clothes that she tried not to fantasize about. The three bullets would be enough for what she had set out to do, but that was it.

The scene was happening a good distance away, but there was something about the boy's face, about his countenance that looked almost alien to Simone. She had seen slaves here die before. Seen free folk die as well, and they almost always had one of two expressions on their faces: fear or defiance. The spectrum of faces that, on one end, sought an escape from death even after its fangs had already sunk their venom, and on the other, embraced it like the teaming up of two enemies to spite a greater foe. Fear or spite. Those were the options and anything in between there. But the young man had neither. It was hard to tell, but even from where she was she thought she could see him making eye contact with her tormentors. And what she saw was a different spectrum, stretched between two different poles. One was a place she herself could only dwell within in absolute solitude: grief. And the other was something that, at this point in her life felt as if it had only been a brief lie she had heard from a long-dead ancestor in a flash of a dream: joy.

The young man slackened.

Simone pictured the man she had killed two month's ago. He had been diseased and covered in boils. To anyone else, he wouldn't have been worth the bullet. Would have probably died less than a week later.

But he hadn't.

She pictured the other three faces, the ones that hadn't yet exploded into the air above their shoulders: one bony obsidian, one thick and freckled with a shock of orange hair.

And one—the last one—pale, muscular, calm.

She had followed all three down the river. Tracked them via word of mouth. Knew where two of them were and would hunt the other until the last of her days.

Obsidian was the one she was waiting for now. He had to be here. She felt it. Sensed it in the tightening of the men's faces. Felt the tension ripple through the starved expressions of the slaves that pressed together in the middle like a herd of prey animals during a dark night when the wind screams and covers the sound of approaching predators.

But she hadn't seen him. Simone had drunk the water that dripped from the ledge above her as the midday sun reached its peak and melted the snow in its thinnest areas. She had slowly eaten the jerky she had tucked up her sleeve, each day eating a little less for fear that she would run out before her task was completed. She had only gotten up to move every six hours, and even then, never actually getting to her feet. She simply pushed herself up and crawled slower than the moon crawls over the sky. It felt good every time, but she doubted she could run if she needed to. That was why she had had to develop her terrifying escape plan.

She soiled herself both physically and psychologically as she lay there devouring her own hatred. If he didn't show his face soon, she would have to resort to plan B: go to him. And even though the camp population wasn't what it had been, she didn't like her odds.

Maybe she could find a way to burn the whole place down. Maybe she would have to flush him out somehow.

But even as she thought the words, the door to the overseer's cabin opened and she realized that it had already been set in motion —that when the young man had thrown himself into the hands of death, he had created a better lure than Simone ever could have.

"Hey," he barked from the doorway. He was so dark that he still drew a silhouette against the deep shadows behind him.

Like some great demon, he emerged from the cabin and walked out into the center of the camp. Simone let the sight hover over his head and tracked him as he walked. His smooth, intentional stride spoke of caution and intelligence. In an age of brutality, Simone was struck by how...*elegant* he looked.

"You like wasting these slaves?" He was tall and impossibly skinny, but when he spoke his voice had the energy that was absent from the famished bodies he resembled. "Get over here."

Simone was too far away to hear him, but as he pointed to the ground in front of him she understood his meaning. The five looked at each other, but none of them moved. Then Obsidian raised one of his arms like some dead tree branch come to life, and pointed at the biggest of the guards. He looked unsure. His face turned rapidly to the others, then up to the dead man beside him, then back over to his master. His steps were slow and tentative at first, but eventually he broke away from the group and made his way forward. The tall man bent down and whispered something in his ear. Simone didn't know what he said, but even from this distance she thought she could see the guard trembling. She breathed in deeply, then exhaled.

Steady.

"This man likes to waste his master's property—likes to waste resources." The tall man was on the verge of yelling now and was slowly turning, addressing the whole camp. "He does not understand that it is he who is being wasted, not the others. This slave-" he pointed at the hanged man, "will be buried. He will become fertilizer in the greenhouse, and he will eventually become the very food you eat. But what of him?" He looked back down at the guard. "How do we make use of a man that is not useful?"

Maybe the guard would have turned to run if he had known what was coming. Maybe he would have begged or reasoned. But it was clear that no matter how much he anticipated his own death, he did not anticipate the means. A bellow of shock and fear began to well in his throat but was immediately cut off as the tall man clamped a hand around his neck, lifted him into the air, and hurled him up and over into the giant cage in the middle of the camp.

"Waste not," the tall man bellowed, even as his words were drowned out by the screams that began to spill forth unrestrained from the guard's lips as the multitude of hungry occupants tore into him and stuffed his raw pieces into their mouths.

Simone had seen enough. She knew the guards would get what they deserved. She knew they'd fall in on each other within the next couple days—knew the proverbial body would flounder and thrash itself to death if she cut off the head.

The wind was blowing from the West. There was no snow in the air. Her line of sight was clear. She snapped the safety off. "Waste not," she mumbled to herself as the obsidian demon strode quickly back to his cabin.

He never made it.

5

JOSHUA

Whenever it came to fight or flight, Joshua chose to fight. Or perhaps "choose" wasn't the right word. He had heard stories of men and women that, though they could almost certainly handle themselves in a fight, had tucked tail and fled when their friends had started to die. Afterward, when they were labeled cowards and questioned why they hadn't stayed to defend their friends, they shamefully admitted that they were scared. They said that by the time it dawned on them that they should stay, they were already shivering down in some far-away ditch long after the violence had ended. They said they hadn't chosen, not really. Their legs had just started moving.

Joshua was not particularly confrontational by nature, but whenever he was threatened directly, his adrenaline would kick him into a hyper-aggressive state. He knew this about himself—knew that he was the type to die for stupid reasons—knew that, in a different time, he would have been the kind of guy to take a bar fight too far or be the man on the evening news who barely remembered killing his wife.

Luckily, his wife hadn't been a very volatile person. They had squabbled and fought occasionally, and there were certain nights when his blood boiled and he had to remove himself from their bed to go sleep on the couch. But they tried to address problems calmly. They almost always worked things out. Almost.

Now, that same adrenaline coursed through him like some holy spirit of wrath and defiance. As the wolves emerged from the shadows, they seemed to bring the shadows with them, and Joshua had to make a choice, or rather, his body chemistry did.

In one quick and fluid motion he drew the handgun from his belt and fired what seemed like a single shot, but then the gun was clicking empty in his hand, and when he tried to think back later on, he thought he remembered firing in such a quick succession that he ran the weapon dry before he even considered aiming. Fear brought him strength, but it seldom brought him clarity.

At least three of rounds hit home. He heard the *smack* of impact and watched one, then another falter. But they resumed their advance. They didn't run but they didn't move slowly either. With long, quick steps they would be on him in seconds, and as soon as the slide on the pistol clacked backward for the last time Joshua turned on his heel and bolted.

He was directionless. No time to reload and he wasn't sure if it would do that much good anyway. So, with the "fight" suddenly flushed from his system, he ran.

A cluster of pine trees lay ahead, the thick branches stretching out to collect falling snow. Joshua's legs were wobbly and he could barely feel them. Too slow. He was moving too slow.

Something ripped by him on the right.

Shit, why couldn't they just get it over with? They were just toying with him now. He thought of how the homesteaders talked about the wolves in the Northern hills. How sometimes they would push one of the herd animals away and circle it until its heart finally gave out. Dead without a single claw mark.

Another movement on his left. He could feel them all around him now—could hear the blood rushing in his ears.

Suddenly his foot caught on a branch or root that must have been underneath the snow and he was falling. Falling as the shadows rushed in to meet him and down he went into the fire. Into the white-hot burning that shook his heart and made his ribs ache as if they were being strummed by some huge and careless angel that hits the strings like so many children when they hold an instrument for the first time.

He sucked in to scream and fire filled his lungs.

GOLDEN SUN STREAMED in through the smudged and mud-speckled window as the truck bumped its way down the gravel road. The man should have been driving—*was* driving, he thought. The vehicle made its way steadily back to its destination, but there were no hands on the wheel. No foot on the gas. The driver's seat was tilted all the way back and the man laid there as if it was the world's most comfortable bed. With his brown Carhartt jacket pulled halfway up his chest, he felt more at ease than he ever had in his life. Steven Tyler was singing over the radio at a volume that was one notch up from silence, so quiet that if he hadn't have known the song, he wouldn't have been able to discern it.

"I know it's everybody's sin, you got to lose to know how to win..."

The man felt like a baby in there, snuggled warmly on his side with his feet curled in like a bean. He had no idea how long he had been like this, only that it was where he wanted to stay.

Who could know if that man was dead or alive? Was the hell from which he had just awoken concrete or was it a contraption forged by his mind and the culminated circumstances that had dropped him on that frozen floor so long ago? Or was it yet to come? Whatever the reality of his situation was, he was here, and in this place of blissful warmth, time wrung its hands of him. Day broke and night fell, but the trapped mortal could not discern any pattern as he rumbled on. Some days felt like they lasted years, while others were momentary flashes of light that almost seemed to lend strength to the darkness that followed. All he knew was that he was moving somewhere, and as he got closer he began to realize where. He wondered what it would take to reach up and turn the wheel down some other road.

But he knew where all those roads led—knew that they all led to the same destination for there was only one road.

The road forward.

JOSHUA WOKE with what felt like a large stone on his chest but when he looked down he found nothing but his wet, sopping clothes. He was cold. Brutally cold. As if instead of snowflakes, one of the black and swollen clouds had dropped a single boulder-sized ball of snow directly on top of him. It wasn't just the cold, he realized, but the soreness. The sharp pains that felt like dancing sparks all throughout his skeleton.

Where was he? The first thing he noticed was the fire that crackled exuberantly next to him. It was set in a stone fireplace and he was so close that it almost hurt. It didn't matter. If he had been any colder there wouldn't have been anything to keep him from trying to stuff the burning logs inside of his coat.

Which was gone...

Crap. Joshua furiously patted his sides. The gun. It was gone, along with the extra magazines, his pouch of food, wool blanket, and every other goddam thing he needed to survive outside. He looked around. He was in a house of some sort. Maybe the owner had his stuff. He doubted it though.

Joshua looked around and tried to remember, but all that came to his mind was a pair of luminous eyes like two headlights.

And running. He remembered running. He remembered the sick,

bile taste of fear that made his legs feel like rubber and his mind incapable of addressing any task that didn't involve brute force.

It must have been the river. Had he fallen in? If he had then he was lucky to have gotten off with a few broken ribs and what felt like a mild case of hypothermia. He had seen men sucked under the surface of that thing like they were wearing lead jackets. He had watched a horse go in and come out in fist-sized pieces over a five-mile stretch. How he had survived he had no clue. And this place...

It was bigger than most houses he'd seen in The Valley, and from the looks of it, far more airtight. It had logs instead of boards, and in place of the typical splintering wood floor lay a heavy slab of stone. He reached down with an arm, still shaking from pain and exhaustion, and placed a tentative hand on it.

"The stone stays warmer than wood if you can heat it consistently." In a doorway stood a short, compact blonde-haired man with a chiseled jaw and kind, blue eyes. "I never liked wood floors. Too scratchy unless you can seal it, and who's making sealer around here?"

Joshua tried to search for the right words, but ended up settling on, "Am I dead?"

"No," the man laughed. "Not any more dead than the rest of us."

Joshua stared uneasily.

"Kidding, you're fine. And very much alive." The man's smile was warm. It didn't beam or radiate, it simply sat there like the glowing coals in the cozy fire beside him. "It was a close one though. I'm on a bend, you see? Got some chain link fence sticking out to catch whatever floats down this way. Mostly just sticks, or pieces of dead things. You're lucky I spotted you though. Was out having a piss. Not much for going inside, ya know. Maybe if I had plumbing but-" he lifted his hands in a *whatcha gonna do* gesture.

"You were pressed up against that fence staring at the sky as if you were waiting for it to fall down on you. So I ran out and hooked you with the hook-stick; drug you in; and then pounded about a hundred gallons of water, muck, and fish piss out of your mouth. Pardon the expression."

"Point is," he pointed a finger at Joshua and he suddenly seemed a lot bigger. "You should be dead." The man's voice had dropped at least an octave into a deep velvet. "So friend, why you out trying to backstroke this time of night?"

Joshua tried to tell him. Tried to remember how he had gotten there—how he had fallen in the river. But as he remembered the details they began to feel so outrageous as to be almost intimate. As if the creatures he had seen hadn't merely happened to him, but were a part of him.

"I was...*pursued*," Joshua explained. The man waited for him to speak further and when he didn't he just nodded.

"Lot of things to chase a man out there. Guess all that needs to be said is: glad ya made it." He smiled and reached out a hand. "Name's Wren." His teeth were the whitest Joshua had seen in over a decade.

Joshua hesitantly—painfully—lifted his hand and shook with his savior. "Joshua," and then after a second he said, "thank you, Wren." The words were soft and alien in his mouth. Not a ton of people to thank down in The Valley.

Wren smiled again and knowingly lowered his voice. "You're welcome." He stood up and stretched. "Well, I suppose we can talk more tomorrow. I reckon you're pretty beat. Won't do you much good to sleep on that stone floor though."

Joshua opened his mouth to say that he was used to it but was cut off.

"Bed's down the hall in the room with the lit lantern. My room's up those stairs." He pointed at a staircase that scaled along the back wall and up through a large square entry hole cut in the ceiling. "You shouldn't hear me clunking around too much. I'm a light sleeper but don't roam like some people do."

Joshua had a million questions: how could he live out here without being pillaged and murdered? Where exactly was he on the river? How the hell did he clean his teeth so well? But all of them instantly evaporated when he heard the word "bed." He hadn't even really acknowledged Wren talking about his room or how light a sleeper he was. Bed. If it was a proper bed—not some stack of sticks and dirt with a blanket on it like most people used—then Joshua hadn't slept in one since...when? He couldn't think that far back. All he knew was that he absolutely had to go see it.

With sudden energy he pushed himself off of the ground, mumbled a "goodnight," and started off towards the hallway.

"Wait a sec," Wren called after him. "Your clothes. They'd probably be best drying out here in front of the fire."

Joshua walked back to the fire, hoping his impatience didn't show, and began to undress.

"I'll give ya some privacy," Wren said as he walked over and began to ascend the stairs. Joshua couldn't give less of a shit about privacy. He ripped every ounce of clothing off and laid it out in front of the fire. Once the clothes were all laid out, Joshua thought for a fleeting second that they looked like they had been worn by a snowman who had come in from outside, laid down in front of the fire, and melted.

Joshua's feet smacked lightly on the stone floor as he strode towards the bedroom. It was a bed. A *clean* bed. It wasn't even soiled in filth like he had half-expected. It looked like his own bed had looked so many years ago. The one he had shared. From deep down inside of him, thoughts he hadn't thought for years began to rise like vomit. He pushed them down.

The bed was queen-size. Or was it king? It had been so long that he didn't think he could tell the difference anymore. The covers were navy blue and lay thickly layered over the top. Two fluffy, white pillows rested at the head like a pair of clouds that had been driven out of the sky by the endless black and gray ones that now occupied it.

Perhaps he was in Heaven. Maybe Heaven was simply access to a bed after living countless years in Hell.

Joshua tentatively lifted the blankets and slipped a leg underneath them. It was like ecstasy. For a second he was afraid that he would be too excited to sleep—too disbelieving in his own luck. What if he just laid there smiling? What if he began laughing, and simply couldn't stop?

But after his ride down the river—after nearly drowning and freezing to death—his body let go. He needn't have worried.

JOSHUA HAD no idea how long he had slept, but when he woke he was so stiff that he thought maybe he had been paralyzed in the night. But bit-by-bit he was able to move his fingers and toes. Then arms and legs. Then finally—painfully—his neck. Then came something else. Pain. All over his body was pain. It wasn't the sharp pain of fractures —though he felt a few of those flare up in his ribs as he lifted himself upright—but the dull hum of bruised muscles, and sure enough, when he looked down at his chest and arms in the light that shone in through the window, his body was a brutal camouflage of yellow and purple.

He laid back down and fell asleep again.

WREN WAS outside splitting wood when Joshua found him. A large log sat upright in the middle of the frosted yard. Atop it was another smaller log that exploded into two pieces as the iron maul landed and delivered its unstoppable blow. Wren was wearing a deerskin coat and pants as he pulled another log from a pile of sawn driftwood to his left. Behind him lay a neatly stacked pile of split firewood.

"How they fit?" he asked without looking up.

Joshua looked down at his own deerskin coat that he had found laid out for him at the foot of his bed. He looked up trying to deter-mine the time of day, and to his surprise, he could see the sun shining clearly above him through a hole in the gray mat of clouds. "Fit's well," he said. He watched Wren lift the maul high above his head and bring it down again with a loud crack. "I don't think I've seen a deer around here in years."

"They're a bit like us," Wren said as he collected the two halves and stacked them with the others. He walked over to the pile of unspilt logs, picked one out, set it up, and raised the maul. "They hate-" Another crack filled the air. "-dying."

Joshua coughed out a laugh. "Yeah, I guess so. I see their tracks now and again. Just too smart to go wandering out in the open I suppose." He looked back up at the sun. "Say, how long was I asleep?"

"About three days." Wren leaned the maul against the splitting log.

Joshua felt dizzy. "Three...three days? How is that..."

"Possible?" Wren took stock of his firewood. "Thought you mighta been dead first. I got you to wake eventually though. Had to feed ya. Walk you to the bathroom. You walked like you'd just fallen off a mountain." He stopped a few feet from Joshua, slipped his hands into his pockets and rocked back on his heels. "Didn't bathe ya though. Figure you'd probably want to do that yourself. Also didn't know how you'd react to water except for the kind that comes out a mug. What with all you've been through."

"I don't remember any of it." Joshua felt lost. "It felt like hours— like dawn should have broken just a few minutes ago."

"Time's funny, aint it? Doesn't work the way we expect it to. Especially here."

"Where is here, by the way? How far down from the mountains are we?"

"Bout-" Wren made a face and tilted a hand. "-twenty miles give or take."

Once again, the ground beneath Joshua's feet felt like it was tilting. *Twenty miles?* He couldn't have been more than five away from the canyon the river exited when he had fallen in. And he knew for a fact that there were rapids between here and there. It wasn't adding up. None of it was.

"Where am I?" he whispered. His eyes met Wren's. "What is this place?"

For the first time, Joshua saw uncertainty in Wren's eyes. Saw pain. And sadness. "You're looking for a way out." It wasn't a question. "Out of The Valley, I mean."

Joshua nodded.

"I mean-" Wren looked down at his feet and made a sour face. "I mean ya gotta know you can't go up the river right? You remember the way in?"

"The rapids are-"

"It's not just the rapids," Wren interrupted. "It's-" He tilted his head back and forth. "You won't make it is all."

"And what's it to you?"

"Nothing. Honestly, it's nothing to me." He pinched the bridge of his nose. "Look, people try to go back up the river all the time. I know because pieces of their boats—of their *bodies*—end up caught in that fence down there."

"You still have those boats?"

Wren blew out a breath. "The *pieces* you mean? Yeah, I keep 'em piled behind the shed over there."

"Big enough to fix?"

"Big enough to make *whole* ya mean? Yeah. Big enough to get you up that river? No. And what would you fix it with?"

"Birchbark, nails, mud, staples, fucking rubber bands. I don't *know*. All I know is that I need to get up that river, and the fact that you don't makes me a little uneasy."

"I can't. I'm stuck here. And so are you." Wren paused a beat. "You been up there?" His eyes flicked Northwest, towards the God's Eye. "Of course you haven't. Because if you had, you'd know what this place was. You'd know who I am. And you'd know that the only way out is to swallow a goddam bullet."

"What is that place?" Joshua was genuinely curious. "What is the God's Eye? People talk about it like its more than just some mountain."

Wren smiled a different smile than he had yet shown, one that made his face look reptilian, like old pictures Joshua had seen of Komodo Dragons. "It's perspective is what it is."

JOSHUA HAD PLANNED on taking at least a week to recover, but nearing the fourth day, he began to get anxious. There was something in the air. A tension pervaded the house and surrounding land, and while he couldn't pinpoint the exact reason, he got the impression that it had something to do with Wren.

It was clear that something about him was abnormal. The nice house, the kind demeanor—how could someone live out here this long? What happened when a group of slavers trundled in? Were they welcomed with the same open arms?

"If you want to try your luck with the river, I can help you," Wren said one night while they cleaned fish they had caught from the stream that afternoon. "I won't go with you, but if you're that determined, I have a canoe that doesn't require that much patchwork. You'll need a wide oar to fight the current, and you'll have to put in a good distance upriver. But-" Wren leaned back and wiped his bloody hands with a rag. "-I know a place that'll give you an advantage."

Still unclear of his motives, Joshua listened. The river was wide and the landscape uneven, which meant that it branched off into several tributaries that ran towards the ocean. Northeast of the forest and before the hills, there was a small stream that branched off of the main river and avoided most of the rapids. People were afraid to use it because it went into a cave and no one was sure where that cave came out. There could have been a massive lake buried in the mountains that dead-ended at some waterfall and whose currents spun you around with no sun or moon to show the way. It wasn't unheard of, and there were plenty of places in those mountains where people entered and simply never came out.

Joshua tried to remember his trip down the river when he had first come to The Valley, but it was hazy. It had happened so long ago, and though it couldn't have taken more than a single night, it felt like it had taken weeks. The lack of stars and immense cloud cover made the darkness so thick had he could have drifted through literally anything and not known it.

He remembered the noises though. He remembered how his torch had gone out and the chirps of crickets were slowly replaced by the deep moans of some distant animals. The flutter of birds erased by the scuttle of claws and the scuff of dragging bellies. He had lain curled up on the raft and squeezed his eyes tight until he awoke to the sound of water turned white upon stone teeth like a snarl from the foaming mouth of some hateful monster. He had abandoned the raft as soon as it swung within a leaps-length of the shore. At that point, he had had no food, no blankets, no weapon—only the longing. The search.

That search had been given up though. Drowned in the despair of having no leads, no direction. No hope. He had followed someone in here, hoping to rescue them, and had gotten lost himself. Now there was only survival and escape.

And it was the escape that Joshua was now focused on. The tributary wound up through the hills and originated half a mile ahead of the main river's mouth. If he made it that far, then maybe there was hope. No one ever made it through the mouth, but what Wren was offering was a chance. A detour.

And it could mean everything.

ON THE MORNING of the fifth day, they checked to make sure the canoe would float. It had had a small wedge-shaped gash on the bottom which they had patched with birch bark and sealed with melted rubber from an assortment of washed-up boots that Wren had been collecting. It wasn't large, but it would be able to carry a single person the length of the river as long as the bottom didn't open on anything.

Another rare advantage he had was the stakes. While rummaging for a suitable oar through a pile of collected junk, Joshua had come across a large metal stake that had likely been used for a stretch of fencing upstream. After some sifting, he had found two more and the heads of each of them had loops through which he could wind a rope. Hopefully, this meant that he wouldn't have to make one continuos journey against the current, but could, at times, secure himself to the river's edge for short periods of time and rest.

When all was said and done, Joshua would be carrying two folded blankets, three pounds of salted fish and dried vegetables, an unlit torch, an extra pair of boots, a serrated hunting knife, the metal stakes, a wooden mallet, a spool of heavy twine, a hatchet, and seventeen .32 caliber bullets that could be used for trading.

To get to the river, it would take almost a full day of walking through forest and rocky terrain. From there he would find a cave to camp in, then at daybreak the following morning he would make the trek up the river.

It would be no small feat if he made it there without running into anyone, but if he could stay alert and keep his distance, he might just make it in one piece.

THE SUN HAD BEEN up for what felt like about two hours when Joshua finally set off. He shook hands with Wren, thanked him for everything, then grabbed the loop of rope attached to the canoe and fastened it loosely around his waist. For the first part of his journey, Joshua would have to pull the canoe like a sled over the snow, so he made sure the rope was good and secure on both ends.

"Be careful with that thing now." Wren was observing Joshua double-check his supplies. "Make sure you don't drag it over any rocks or anything."

Joshua still found himself thrown off by Wren's manner of speech. Most people he came across chose as few words to say as possible, as if language was just as valuable a commodity as food and clothing. "Shouldn't be a problem. The furs should blunt any sharp edges." Instead of laying bare upon the snow, the canoe had four heavy, fur blankets fastened to the bottom, the last of which had a thin layer of rubber melted to it to reduce friction as it was being dragged.

"Why don't ya take these as well?" Wren asked

Joshua was so surprised when he saw the tiny box that he thought it might be some trick—that upon sliding the tiny cardboard container open he would find nothing but a fistful of tiny twigs. So it was with great care that he slowly pushed the end of the box to reveal a neat little bunch of waterproof matches, packed tightly like a massive extended family all sleeping in a single bed. He swallowed. He wanted to say something. Wanted to show his gratitude. But in the end, he just gave a nod and slid the box gently into the inside flap of his coat pocket.

Matches hadn't been seen in The Valley since he had been there. He usually had to make do with odd pieces of flint and tiny shaved piles of birch bark. With matches, he could...could...

For one crazy second, he saw The Valley in flames. Every tree was a pillar of ash. Every last inch of snow was transformed into an extension of the mighty river so as to drown the world in fire and baptize it in an apocalyptic flood. What would the new arrivals find? A field? A giant skating rink? It didn't matter. All that mattered was that they would find it empty. And empty...was good.

Joshua shook himself. There were times when he understood the old tale of Prometheus. The god that had stolen fire from the heavens and given it to man, only to be chained to a mountaintop as punishment and devoured every day until the end of time. What would happen on the day that man had perished—that fire was returned to the gods? Would Prometheus finally be relieved of his torment? Or would the silence of a dead race stand as a testament to the folly of man and the power of fire, ringing a hollow death knell on into eternity as if to blame that single act of mercy for the ruin of all?

"Where'd ya go there bud?" Wren looked concerned and questioningly at Joshua.

"Sorry," Joshua exclaimed. "Been a while since I held something like this."

"You had the gun didn't ya? Might as well have been the same thing," he laughed.

Joshua gave a chuckle. "For all the good it did me," he said almost to himself.

The two shook hands, making Joshua uncomfortable one last time, and then they finally parted. It wouldn't be until that evening, as Joshua stuck his hand in his pocket to feel for the matches, that he would realize that he had never told Wren about the gun.

6

THE PACK

That evening, a smattering of broken clouds and dense atmosphere took hold of the sun's rays and wrung them bloody and bright, so as to make the western sky look like a giant wound in a doomed world. The Pack had dispersed after they saw the body slip below the serrated surface of the river. He should have been dead, but they could still smell him in the snowy air. They had failed to attain vengeance, thus making their hunger for it that much more ravenous, as if his escape was but another slight against them.

They had come across a small caravan of slaves the day before and all had knelt in melting supplication. Hair fizzling and skin boiling and popping, their destruction had been a mere distraction. A game, in which the odds were stacked so high against them that they possessed no option but to step into the volcanic jaws.

They had all been guilty to be sure, but there were others more suited for punishment. Like the man. Only a couple degrees of separation removed, he was a more appropriate prey. And the fact that he was so *close*. It made him practically irresistible.

No sign of the other. But his time would come.

The man had been tough. Not old, but not young either. Grizzled and silver-streaked, he was like one of the wary deer that preferred solitude over the herd and stuck to the deepest and most remote parts of the forest.

But now he was on the move. Was *still* on the move. They could still *feel* him. He had lived somehow, and now that they had been so close his death was nigh unstoppable. They simply had to find him.

The sun rose and fell six times as they spread out and made their way slowly down the river, combing thoroughly for sign. It was as the last crimson sliver of light was extinguished that they rose like mist at the door.

WREN WAS SITTING IN A COMFORTABLE, leather chair reading a worn paperback copy of *The Sound and the Fury* when he heard the three sharp knocks at his front door. There was at least a modicum of relief in knowing that they had missed Joshua, even if his quest was doomed in the end. Wren had sent him Northeast on purpose, calculating the speed at which The Pack was moving along the river. But it was ultimately up to Joshua to determine his speed of travel, thus placing the disguised choice of life and death in his hands. And the fact that The Pack was here now meant that they had indeed missed him.

A wall of cold air blasted in as Wren opened the door, and suddenly he was surrounded on all sides. He hadn't seen them or heard their steps. They were simply there. Their entrance was intangible and edge-less like the beginning of a nightmare.

"Where is he?" The large one with the yellow eyes asked calmly. They were people by all outward appearances. Two men and two women. All of them with the same honey-brown skin and oil-black hair. Certain facial features were repeated in a few of them so as to confirm a blood relation, of which Wren was already aware.

"He's here. In The Valley. He's still within reach, and will remain so as long as he continues to search in the manner he has chosen."

"You let him sleep here. Fed him. Healed him. Why?" The words came from a woman missing her left eye. Impatience had snuck into her voice. They all stood stock-still.

"The same reason you're still tracking mud all over my goddam floor, it serves no purpose to kill someone here." He shrugged his shoulders and rolled his eyes. "And I get bored. What you do though...is interesting..."

"Stop lying," the large one snapped. "We found the old man. The one he killed. Don't try and convince us that killing him will be fruitless. Death is the *only* fruit here."

Wren smiled. "Fruitless for me, I mean. You are correct. Death still breathes in The Valley."

"Where did he go?"

The circle around Wren tightened, the figures hunched and stiff.

"He will be moving Northwest," Wren said. "He will seek The God's Eye. You can still catch him if you leave immediately."

There was a moment of silence before the big one motioned towards the door. "You better be right." He stood aside for the other three to exit. After the others had left he turned back towards Wren. "What's your part in this? And don't try and sell me any bullshit about being lonely."

Wren smiled his warm smile. "Perspective," he said simply.

The big man in the doorway smiled wide, exposing his massive canines.

ONCE OUTSIDE, the smaller of the two men turned toward's the leader. "North?"

"No," he said. "Never trust a word out of that one's mouth. We go

Southwest. He has tried to cross the tundra twice before. He will try again."

In the short time it took The Pack to interrogate their subject, a mass of clouds had swept in off of the ocean, bearing huge amounts of snow. The moon hung mute and cold in the sky. A dead eye staring naked in all directions, seeing nothing and knowing less.

7

OVIN

Empty shells rained upon the street like autumn leaves from a shaken tree. Each round cylinder of brass caught the sunlight and reflected amber in every direction like a shimmering golden waterfall cascading over smooth rocks into a tropical paradise far below. The pile widened and grew on the ground like an ancient pyramid being built on fast forward. Each brick a hollow cloak having already exhausted death to be placed upon one another. A massive tomb composed of countless smaller ones.

"Fuck, Ovin, you fired that thing so long it looked like the chamber was having a piss on the pavement."

Ovin ducked back behind the wall, breathing hard. "Yeah, how 'bout you help out here instead of waiting for my head to get blown off."

Bullets had begun to ping against the dumpster they were crouched behind. If the bastards were using handguns or shotguns they should be fine. There was enough junk and scrap metal inside to slow a pistol round even if it went through, assuming they were using hollow points. If they were using full metal jackets or rifle rounds though it'd be a different story. Ovin didn't trust the thing regardless. They had to move.

Ovin, Russ, and Stewart had been out looking for Trixie when they were ambushed by gunfire from the surrounding buildings. The place was supposed to be a dead zone. Windows were boarded shut, shops closed down. The town had seen so much violence that almost everyone had fled. Even so, Ovin had pushed for their small group to avoid traveling on the streets. It was too open, no matter how many alleys were close enough to duck down.

They had no idea they were being watched until Stewart's knees, thighs, and lower abdomen got shredded all up and down the street. He might have still been alive for all Ovin knew, but there wasn't an occupied hospital for miles, and no one back at camp could treat such a grievous set of wounds. Chances were he was already in shock and about two pints from crossing the line of no return.

Fuck him. And fuck his dog too. The dogs left in the pack were still more than enough to get the job done. And that was what was important right now: the job. They had to find their target. They had been hot on his trail for a long time now. Jumping from town to town. Always a day late. A step behind.

A short burst of fire ripped into the dumpster Russ and Ovin were crouched behind, and now Ovin was looking at three new beams of light stretching out from fresh bullet holes.

"We need to get the fuck out of here," Russ said. He couldn't have been more than twenty, and why he was here was a complete mystery to Ovin.

"Obviously," Ovin said flatly. "There a reason you didn't run down the opposite alley like we had planned?"

"I don't know man. I panicked." Russ compulsively wiped a lock of blonde hair from his eyes.

"The plan was in place for you to default to when you *did* panic. So either you weren't listening, or you have a hot and burning desire to die right here next to me."

"They'll come for us though, right? I mean, Trent and them?"

"No. We're on our own. That's what they said. In fact, I'm not even sure why *I'm* here. Should have let Stewart find his own damn dog. "

"I thought you liked Trixie," Russ said questioningly.

Ovin did like Trixie. In fact, she was his favorite of the pack, but he wasn't about to let Russ know that. "How about we stop talking about the dog for a second and let me think."

The alley was a dead end. A few windows peered out from the second floor but they were too high to reach, at least by himself.

"Hey Russ, I know you're new, but you ever fired a gun before?"

"Dammit man, of course I've fired a gun before. How'd you think I-"

"Ok," Ovin cut him off. "We haven't fired for a little too long now, which means they're probably working their way over here. What I need *you* to do, is to go brace your back up underneath that window. While you're doing that I'm going to use my last magazine to provide some covering fire. Then I'm going to run over and you're going to pop me up through that window."

"Which window?" Russ interrupted.

"The only window that doesn't have half-a-million goddam boards nailed over it. Looks like the glass has already been busted out, so it should be cake, got it?"

Russ nodded.

"Then, you're going to throw me that embarrassingly full M4 you have slung around your back."

"But-"

"Don't worry. You'll still have your sidearm." Ovin gestured at the Beretta Russ had strapped to his thigh. "Don't shoot unless they come around that corner. We need to time this perfectly so that, as they start to move in, I can swing around behind them and catch them out in the open. Got it?"

Russ nodded uncertainly.

"Ok." Ovin dropped his empty magazine, stuffed it into his ruck-sack, and replaced it with his last full one. "Go."

THE FIRST PART WENT WELL. Ovin aimed his rifle blindly over the dumpster, depressed the trigger until it was empty, slung it over his shoulder, ran the short distance to Russ, put his right foot into his cupped hands, and was launched through the window. It was when he reached down to receive Russ's weapon and found him already running back to his spot behind the dumpster that things went awry.

Ovin was on the brink of yelling after him when he realized that it would almost definitely give his position away. The *pop-pop-pop* of Russ's rifle began, which meant the clock had started ticking.

Shit, shit, shit. Ovin had to move *right now.* There was a fury to Russ's bursts that suggested to anyone listening that he was about two-seconds from breaking down on the spot.

The room Ovin had jumped into was cramped, dusty, and grossly overdecorated. All over the walls hung bright paintings and knits; and tucked into the window-side corner was a cluttered table with a few empty, clay mugs on it. As quick as he could, Ovin unclipped everything that rattled or made noise, including his rifle and ruck-sack. After unburdening himself, he drew the Glock 17 from his thigh holster, pulled the slide half-way back to make sure there was a shell in the chamber, and then made his way over to the door. The person who had lived here must have left in a hurry and not planned on coming back, because the door's accumulation of locks and bolts hadn't been engaged, allowing Ovin to quietly turn the knob and exit the room.

The building was a small living complex that had tight hallways and steep stairs. Checking his corners as he went, Ovin made his way quickly to the roof where he could get a better perspective of what was going on. When he got to the door however, he discovered it was locked, spun around, and immediately descended back down. There had been no place around the door to stash a key and shooting the lock would have surely given him away. Not to mention the fact that he had a better chance of injuring himself than he had of actually blowing the lock off. He'd have to take his chances in the streets. There was probably a door leading to the neighboring complex, but his failure to exit onto the roof had drained precious seconds. Russ might already be dead.

For a second, Ovin thought of running. He could leave Russ to be shot or abducted. If the kid was smart he'd fight tooth and claw to avoid capture, even if it meant dying. If these were the people Ovin thought they were, then surrendering only meant one thing: torture. But if *Russ* was the person that Ovin thought he was, he was sure that he would give himself up at the drop of a hat. How the hell did he find himself here?

There was no time to think about it. Ovin slipped through the stairwell door and into the lobby, swept the room, crouched, and made his way as quickly as he could over to the entrance. There was a small counter dug into the South wall and a tiny doorway that most likely led to a cramped, little office. The door Ovin was now pressed against was sturdy and thick, but had a small window at the top that looked as if it had had its glass busted in. Ovin listened. He heard the scratching sound of footsteps nearby, which meant they were out in the street. He'd have to be fast. The Glock wasn't ideal but if they were close enough and not wearing body armor he had a chance. He braced himself.

Without warning, the stairwell door through which Ovin had just come through clattered open and he leveled his automatic at the man who entered—baring what looked like a crude and rusted shotgun— and fired twice into his chest. The *pock-pock* of the 9mm rounds was loud, but Ovin had been conditioned to not even think about it, which—with the assistance of the adrenaline pumping through his veins—was hardly difficult. Before considering the consequences he spun, yanked the front door open to reveal two armed men in the streets who were already turning towards him, and shot the closest one center mass.

He could have tried for the second, but he instinctively ducked behind the door as a spray of machine-pistol fire ripped through the space he had just occupied. Thankfully, the door was so heavy that it absorbed most of the bullets without coming apart, which couldn't be said for the walls on either side. It looked as if the building had originally been constructed out of brick, but Ovin guessed that in later years the front wall had been torn down and extended to create a lobby with what looked like some sort of particle board, which was now more particle than it was board.

Ovin felt it. Felt the heat rising in his chest. It was the feeling that made him feel bulletproof—that turned enemies into prey. He looked at the downed man that lay half in the stairwell and at the dark pool around him that seemed more black then red. Ovin breathed, dipping into an old memory. He would get one shot at this.

Suddenly another frequency of gunfire filled the air, this one deeper and further away. Ovin spun around the door, aimed at the man's body that had already begun to ripple from the other shots, and pulled the trigger.

This time Ovin was completely aware of everything. The minute amount of pressure required to squeeze the trigger. The internal mechanism that hit the center of the cartridge, primed the gunpowder, and propelled the small piece of lead out of the muzzle of the barrel. The gases from the explosion sending the weapon's slide back to eject the empty shell and replace it with a fresh one in the chamber, but long before that new round would lay snug at the back of the tube, its predecessor would fly through the air like a comet, and catch the right side of the man's temple as he turned slower than the dawning of an age. The hollow point would mushroom as it impacted upon his skull—the skull that, as a young child, had come together like the tectonic plates of a sentient world—and a furious storm of lead fragments would collect bone and brain matter like a congregation of gory disciples that would then be carried on a fatalistic path out through the other side of the man's head. In the space between the head and the building's wall on the other side of the street where the bullet would make its home, wet pieces of white bone would fall upon the street like stars upon the earth.

The man crumpled.

Ovin noticed two things: that the two dead men in the street were not wearing body armor, and that the kid's gunfire had not been met with return fire.

"We *got* em." Russ was all but jumping for joy as he ran over.

Ovin scanned the windows. "We need to leave." For a second he considered going back into the housing complex to retrieve his supplies, but decided against it. "The gunfire might lure more of them, so we need to go *now*." He jotted over to where Stewart lay in the street since the beginning of the attack, grabbed his rifle and pack, found his wallet, stuffed it in his pocket, and jogged back over to Russ. "And this time, we don't take the streets."

"Ok, but—hey, Ov?"

Ovin turned to glare at him. "What."

With a sheepish look, Russ said, "Sorry about not handing you the gun."

The whole way back, Ovin resisted the urge to stab him in the neck, and throw him down a goddam well.

"So Stewart's gone then?"

"Yeah." Ovin ate from an unheated can of corn.

Russ and Ovin had returned just before nightfall to the makeshift camp that was dug into the base of a hill just two miles from town. As soon as they had arrived, Russ declared that he "absolutely had to go lay down on his cot before he did anything else." Adrenaline hangover. So be it, there were a few things Ovin wanted to ask Trent anyway. Like why in the holy hell was Russ there in the first place.

"And you don't think they were Espina's boys?"

"No." Ovin swallowed the last mouthful of cold corn, let the spoon clatter into the empty can, and set it down on the table. "I thought so at first, but they didn't have any gear except for one machine pistol, a lever action rifle, and what looked like a single-shot shotgun. They attacked all at once and from the same direction, so they hadn't had any training. Or, if someone did loop around to hit us from behind, they were lacking firepower and decided to hightail it out of there once their buddies got smoked. So my guess: they were probably just locals. Maybe bandits, maybe not. Doesn't really matter."

"Trixie came trotting back twenty minutes after y'all left ya know?" A smile flickered on Trent's face but in the next instant it was gone. They'd lost one of their own.

"Yeah, that fucking figures."

Trent nodded. A man of about forty, he had a full beard that still contained more brown than grey, intelligent hazel eyes, and a patient and calm demeanor. He had been Ovin's CO ever since they'd begun the hunt, and the only man he could come to with questions, so he asked one now.

"Russ." Ovin gave him a hard stare. "What the fuck?"

Trent smiled and nodded. "Yeah, I was just about to ask you about that. How'd he do?"

"Exactly how you'd expect him to, what with him being a *child* and all. C'mon man, we're not the army. How's someone like that wind up with us?"

Trent furrowed his brow. "That's funny. I seem to remember a seventeen year old falling in with us back in the day. Seemed to turn out ok."

"Yeah, I had spent five years on the *streets*. That kid looks like he just spent the last five years inside his Grandma's basement playing Pac-Man. Boy's so soft I thought he was gonna be dog food until you handed him a rifle."

"Truth?" Trent scratched his head looking little uncomfortable. "He's Cruz's kid."

"Ah, what the fuck? He not want us to do our jobs? He trying to sink this thing?"

"Sorted something out with Danewitz. Not sure if he wants the kid to become a man or a corpse. Probably doesn't care, as long as its one or the other."

"Shit." Ovin went to smack the empty tin can off of the table but remembered who he was sitting with.

"Good news though." Trent lifted his eyebrows in mock excitement. "Got a line on one of Espina's main groups. They're a kill squad that operates up North, out of the valley. Call themselves *El Paquete*."

"The Pack?" Ovin asked.

Trent nodded.

Ovin leaned forward as Trent pulled out a map, pointed to their current position, and then traced a long line with his finger up the paper towards a blank spot near the ocean.

"This isn't an intel run. They operate cold. Only dead drops. This is going to be shock and awe. Fear and intimidation. Cruz want's Espina pissing himself before we give the final tightening of the noose."

"So," Ovin cracked his knuckles. "We using the dogs then?"

Trent gave a wolfish smile and for the first time that night, Ovin thought he looked nothing short of demonic.

8

SIMONE

Simone's rifle was a .308 caliber Remington 700 with a Walnut stock and iron sights. It had proven its ability to end a life, and now if she couldn't work fast enough right here at this very moment, it would end hers as well.

When Simone pulled the trigger there was an immensely brief period of time from when the weapon fired and when the bullet stopped. But in this short window, she had watched the tall, thin man turn his head impossibly fast. It was as if he had heard the shot and reacted to it while the bullet was still in the air, which was impossible, of course. Simone knew from a lifetime of shooting that bullets traveled faster than sound. Still though, right as the gun bucked in her hand, she could have sworn she saw him tense, turn, and face her.

It had not been enough. Her third-to-last round had shorn the top-half of his head off, and he fell to the ground like a pile of blackened bones.

No one knew where the shot came from, but they probably would soon. Simone slid backward and slung the rifle over her shoulder. It was empty, but that was good. If it were loaded she might be tempted to use it to defend herself, and if she did that then she wouldn't have any more ammunition left to finish the job. It was a risk, but one she was willing to take. All that mattered was killing the other two.

"Up there," someone shouted, and Simone knew she had been spotted.

Fifty feet down, the path branched into two sections, one that continued down to the bottom and another that swung up, over, and along the cliff that lay on the opposite side of the mountain Simone had dug into. Some men were already climbing the steep rock and would soon meet Simone at the fork. She had to make it there before they did.

A gunshot rang out and rock splinters exploded in front of her face. Dammit, she didn't think they had any firearms or ammunition left. Another bang, but it also went wide.

Simone ran with a rigid gait, her legs wobbling beneath her. Every step was both painful and powerless, but fear and purpose coursed through her and pushed her forward.

The bottom of an old t-shirt she had cut apart had been hanging around her neck, but now she pulled it up to cover her face, the long, black dreadlocks that hung down the back of her head were already tied and stuffed into her coat: they couldn't know she was a woman. That fact would make them more...*motivated.*

The path was slippery and she almost lost her footing more than a few times. Her body quaked with fatigue. *Just a few more feet.*

One man had a lead on the others, and he pulled up short of the fork, drew a fat little revolver out from under his coat and aimed it at her. "Stop," he shouted. He was too close to miss unless he was bluffing and didn't *actually* have any bullets in the gun. He glanced back to see how far the others had to reach him and it was clear that he wanted Simone for himself. She had no illusions about their loyalty to the man she had just killed. She was an outsider, and they were hungry.

Simone tried not to think about the fact that their leadership was gone and what that now meant for the slaves down there. There'd be time for that later.

"Stop!" The man yelled again. They'd take her alive if they could, but there wasn't any great incentive to do so anymore. Sure, they could keep a captor for a little while longer than they could a dead person, but in the end, it would dawn on them that the shit was about to hit the fan and that there would be no prisoners. There would be no survivors except for those that proved strong enough—those that showed they wouldn't be worth trying to kill.

Simone saw his body tense in anticipation of the recoil. Her feet landed on a wide stone that lay at the intersection of the three paths, and as soon as she began to pivot, she realized too late that this is when he would stake the shot. She had messed up. Blown it.

She squeezed her empty fists in anticipation.

If it were to be heard from a distance, it would have sounded like nothing more than a tiny pop. And the long wail that followed sounded more like that of defeat than pain.

WHEN THE GUNPOWDER IGNITED, the bullet exploded away from the metal cartridge that had once held it. In addition to this, pieces of the cylinder exploded away from the frame, splinters of barrel flew in every direction; a thumb and a chunk of index finger spun away from each other, and fragments of the revolver's hammer and handle flew backward towards thin lips, flushed cheeks, and a pair of wet and open eyes.

The bullet plowed into the snow six feet behind Simone, and when she heard the man scream she realized that he must have had the wrong sized cartridge in the gun. If the cartridge was too small it would have room to expand within the chamber and act more like a small grenade then a bullet.

She hurtled up the path and swung around the rock just as the screaming man fell to his knees in the snow, bloody and blinded. Her other pursuers were too far behind to see what happened next, but maybe that was for the better. As she turned the corner of the cliff, one of her shaky legs finally gave way. Her boot slipped and she tried to grasp the stone ledge. She failed.

The snow below is too wet, she thought fleetingly as she began to fall.

It wasn't the heavy, sticky snow that she had used to build snowmen when she was little, but the kind that made the top layer stick together—that, after a cold night, would freeze into a thick and icy crust.

The cliff sloped rather than plummeted, so she didn't drop straight down as much as bounce hard on her butt and back and tumble into an uncontrolled fall.

Pain screamed through her where she had hit, the sky and ground flashing before her eyes as she spun downwards. This was it. After all of this—all of the waiting and preparation—she was going to die in a ridiculously clumsy move. She had killed her target just to turn and run off of a cliff. And even if she survived, then what? Would she just lay there crippled and wait for them to crest the hill, look down at her, laugh, and then just drop a big fucking rock on her head?

She had been so absorbed with the kill—the act of vengeance— that the time and effort she had devoted towards fantasizing about it should have been spent thinking of a better escape plan. One that didn't involve trying to outrun a dozen grown men on her weakened legs.

Mercifully, she landed on her back and the impact was distributed against her body. She hit with a soft *wump* and sunk a foot-and-a-half into the pile of snow. For a second Simone, just laid there as small rocks and bits of snow pattered around her. Grey clouds hung overhead like an abstract, monochromatic watercolor painting. It was beautiful. Dark flowed into light and then back again in seamless transition, making it look like a gently roiling sea without depth, and in a sense it was. She knew that above her stretched an expanse that, if she were to be unhooked from the earth's gravity, she could push herself up and forward and fly unimpeded for all of eternity.

She glanced at the steep spot where she had slipped.

Faces swam into her vision. Faces that couldn't be there. Ones that had long since dissolved into the ground beneath. Would she see them now? Would vengeance matter? Would justice?

Cries came from above as she watched what looked like men, but could just have easily been women, crest the rock on the side of the cliff. Where had she gone, she imagined them thinking. All they had to do was look down and see her. She thought about trying to run but exhaustion was like an endless barrage of ocean waves through her body. She had thought that slow stretching and exercise would keep her muscles in shape for the three days she had laid there. She had been wrong. She was *so tired*. So...defeated.

A man shouted to the rest of the others climbing the hill. Simone couldn't make out what he had said, but he sounded frustrated. Someone shouted at him from just a few feet away. A woman. The acoustics were such that everything they said was close to being just indistinguishable noise, but she caught the word "cliff," and "bottom."

But as the man tried to turn around to look down, his foot slipped and Simone saw a big rock the size of her chest come loose. The man had fallen down but not off. His one leg hung over the edge as he tried to push himself back up. He, however, was now the least of Simone's concerns.

Her eyes widened as she watched the giant rock drop and bounce down the side of the cliff. It struck in multiple places and where it did she could see huge sheets of snow break away from the surface and begin to slide down towards her. *Crack. Crack. Crack.* The rock bounced again and again, breaking off smaller pieces of rock under-neath the snow. And finally, it plummeted one last time.

The displaced air made a sound like someone sucking in a breath as the rock landed four feet to the left of Simone's head, and right as the others began to look down to where the rock had fallen, Simon pressed her eyes shut as a massive torrent of snow came barreling down the hill and landed right on top of her.

SIMONE WAS BURIED. She had imagined being buried—being nestled into a mountain, how couldn't you?—but when she did she had pictured it being white all around. Which was silly, of course. How could any light get in? Even so, she couldn't have imagined it would be so *dark*. She could have been a mile below the ocean's surface and she wouldn't have known any different. In a way, she supposed she was.

Nothing more happened that she could tell. No more falling rocks. No bullets cutting through the snow and into her body.

Then her lungs began to burn.

Simone had to get out. She had no idea how much snow was on top of her but she had to find a way up and through, but when she moved her arms they felt like they were glued in place. *Maybe I'm still just tired. Still weak.* But the shrill alarm bells of panic had begun to ring in her head. *I have to move. I have to move. I have to*—Simone began to twist her body back and forth. Her arms had been at her sides but now she was making a small amount of space for them to move around—to punch through the snow above her. It was wet and cold on her face, but she still felt hot tears burn their way out of her eyes as she started to cry in frustration. Her lungs were throbbing; two huge, sore muscles in her chest. With what breath was left inside of her she screamed soundlessly into the snow and began thrashing as melted ice water began to run into her mouth. She tried to scream again but there was nothing left.

Simone's mind was so ravenous that at first, she failed to register the lack of resistance against the fingers on her right hand, but something cut through the blaze in her mind, some high note of logic was just barely audible over all of the chaos.

It said, *stop waving your hand. They might see it.*

She had broken through. Her hand had broken through the top and when she pulled it back a stream of light speared down through the hole and blinded her. Simone gulped air. Her lungs expanded and contracted in ecstasy as they pumped oxygen back into her blood and delivered it to the rest of her body. She had done it. She had lived.

Now she just hoped that no one had seen her hand. However merciful and glorious the hole was, it still wasn't close enough for Simone to see anything except for the sky directly above her. What if someone came and looked down it? What if they just dumped an armful of snow back down? Fear froze her in her place. Not that she could move particularly well yet, but at this point in time she just hoped that her little tunnel up into the world of the living would go unnoticed.

She closed her eyes and counted to herself.

I hope they don't have dogs, she thought.

She was *sure* they didn't have any dogs. There were no mealtimes which meant that they were down to scrounging. Any dogs would have been eaten by now. But still, if there *were* dogs they would lead them right to her. Of course, they would have to go down and around a few giant mounds of rock to get to the bottom of the cliff, but Simone wasn't fully convinced that they wouldn't try. What she was betting on right now was that there was no longer anyone to punish them for what they did with the slaves. They would be much easier prey.

Simone finally allowed herself to think about them and it made her feel sick. All of those people down there were doomed—doomed because of her. In murdering their master, she had removed the only thing protecting them from being killed, cooked, and eaten. Those people—the slavers—they didn't give a shit about the slaves. They were there because of fear. They didn't trust the settlements, the homesteads. They didn't think they could make it on their own. The fear of death warped them into monsters willing to do anything to survive, and the men that Simone currently hunted were the facilitators. They were the promise that those who followed and obeyed would be protected.

Some of the slavers were terrified of those men. Of Obsidian. Of the man with the fiery beard. Of...*him.* The men who bowed to them were nothing more than slaves themselves. Bound and shackled by threats. Caged by the acts they had witnessed.

Guilt surged through Simone. Guilt and sadness. Sadness for the slaves—for the slavers *and* the guards. Sadness for everyone but the two she hunted, and the two she had already killed. She remembered the face of the boy that had hung himself. Remembered his expression and how foreign it was. Regret? Resignation?

It didn't matter. She tried to push it out—tried to focus on counting. Still though...

She would need supplies. Food, most of all. She was almost out and could feel the dry throb of hunger in her belly. The camp would be of no use even if she could magically find a way in. Caravans with supplies had been infrequent in her observations and those that came to buy slaves typically traded with coins. When it came to slave camps, enough people with food had it simply taken from them by the guards, and it got to the point where no one would go near any settlement of any kind with food in their possession except for The Harbor.

The Harbor was a settlement by the ocean that tried to sell itself as a sort of safe-haven, which it sort of was as long as you didn't mind being robbed, raped, or stabbed to death. It was relatively untouched by the slave trade though, as it dealt more in fish than anything else. Slavers had been trying to move in for as long as anyone could remember, but since its inception, it had been guarded against any organized forces by armed militia members. People wanted somewhere they could feel safe. Some chose to defend homes, some chose to keep moving and travel alone, and some preferred to let others protect them. The last of these resided in The Harbor.

Simone was a long way from The Harbor however, and she felt anything but safe.

SIMONE HAD TRIED to count to 25,000, which she figured would allow enough time for the darkness of night to descend. But somewhere around 2,000, exhaustion had taken hold and she had drifted off. Now—panic-stricken—her eyelids flew open and were filled with snow. Where was she? What time was it? She felt like she had been frozen almost all the way through, and when she tried to move she discovered that she couldn't. Not immediately, at least. First, she just wiggled in the dark like a newborn worm. Her clothes scrubbed against the snow around her and needles pricked her hands and feet. Eventually though, she began to make progress. She pushed her shoulders back and forth, kicked her legs forward and pulled them back. Finally, she was able to lift her hands to her face and dig her way up.

There was only a few feet on top of her, and soon she was able to thrust her head out into the dark night air. She stopped and listened, her head throbbing. Nothing.

Had they gone already? Had they eaten the slaves like she had thought they would?

Simone's stomach roiled in a repulsive contradiction of revulsion and hunger. No, she didn't want to know. She pulled herself the rest of the way out of the snow, brushed herself off, and took a few tentative steps forward.

She could barely move.

As she continued away from camp however, blood began to flow back into her body. Her steps became quicker and more assured. Her stride lengthening, her breathing evening out. She made her way up over the smaller hill that lay opposite the cliff she had fallen from.

From there she found the trail she had scouted days before and followed for about a mile up, down, and around jagged and jutting stones that lay buried in earth and snow. Eventually, the ground began to level out as the trail swung South, and before long she was entering an open, big-timber forest. The trees were so tall they looked like they ascended into the darkness infinitely.

She slowed down and looked around. It was easy to get lost in a place like this, especially in the dark, but the moon was a little brighter than usual and the snow glowed a dark silver all around. It was quiet. It was also cold, but not as cold as some nights. In fact, it almost felt like it was above freezing, the snow wet and formable under her boots. Simone turned slowly, her eyes prying apart the darkness.

There.

To her left, a couple hundred feet away, was a dark wall of black where the snow simply stopped. Simone trudged over to it; confirmed that it was the large, stone overhang that she thought it was; and started making her way alongside it.

The cave was so well hidden in shadow that she almost passed it the first time. In fact, she almost certainly would have if she hadn't recognized the large fallen tree she had to hop over a short distance ahead of it. But she did, and with great relief, she stepped inside, fumbled around for the bag she had hidden there, and finally pulled out a small wooden box that contained pieces of flint and stone. She then walked ten paces into the cave, her hand against the wall, and found the fire she had built with the edge of her foot. Sparks flew from the stone and flint and caught easily on the dry tinder and birchbark that lay underneath the wood she had piled.

The cave became illuminated with the dancing reds and oranges of the fire, the heat feeling as if it had been sent from Heaven.

After warming herself for a while, Simone unslung the bag and rifle from around her shoulders. The barrel of the rifle was almost surely clogged so she sat down and painstakingly disassembled the entire thing. Her hands were still cold so it took a little longer than usual, but the steps had become routine and soon enough she found herself working at a steady pace. There was a cleaning kit inside of her pack and she withdrew it and used the tiny rod and cloth to scrub about a foot-and-a-half's worth of snow and dirt out from inside the barrel.

After cleaning and oiling the entire gun, she reassembled it, withdrew one of the remaining rounds, snapped it into the magazine, pushed the magazine up into the rifle, and then slid the bolt forward and down to secure the round in the chamber.

Two down, two to go.

Now for the scary part.

A large tin can sat by the fire and Simone picked it up, strode outside and filled it with snow. The burning wood crackled and popped as she nestled the can up against it. She had a few more empty cans, and not wanting to constantly refill the big one, she filled the others with snow as well and lined them up around the fire.

Simone removed the spare clothing from her pack and placed it on the ground in front of her. The canvas bag was close to empty now so she smoothed it out, slipped out of her boots and filthy socks, stepped gingerly onto the pack, and finally leaned over and dropped the cloth that hung around her neck into the big can of melting snow. She couldn't tell in the low firelight, but her feet looked bad. Patches of dead skin hung here-and-there and her nails looked as if they could fall off at any moment.

Moving quickly now, she took off her jacket and let it fall to a pile on the rough, stone floor; then she peeled off the rest of her clothing.

Those three days had not been kind to her. Dead skin and much, much worse hung grotesquely off of every inch of her dark body. In addition, she could now see her ribs for the first time in a long time, and come to think of it, she thought her tailbone might be fractured from the fall. She had no doubt that if someone were to turn the corner and see her corpse-like body lit up in the crimson firelight they would think her some sort of risen devil.

Tears welled up in her eyes, and suddenly it all came forth. The death, the hunger, the wasteland she inhabited. The blood she had spilled, whether by inaction or her own hands. The faces of the people gone from her life forever, those that she missed so much she thought it would literally crush her like a stone. And finally, almost as if it had forgotten to surface until the final moment, the young boy's eyes. She hadn't been close enough to see them, but she thought she could see them now. Dark brown gateways into a world she couldn't fathom, set feebly within a failing body, hovering over a doomed land.

Simone sobbed into the back of her hands as she slowly knelt to the ground. A cold wind blew gently in and caressed her naked body like a curious specter. She shivered.

She had disrobed with the intention of putting her spare set of clothes on, but now she didn't have the energy, nor did she want any sort of fabric touching her skin. Slowly and arduously, she withdrew the cloth from the big tin can of water that was now unevenly warm and began to clean herself. She was lost in a trance. Dipping, wringing, wiping, scrubbing. She became warmer as she became cleaner, the fire close enough to make it feel as if she would catch at any moment. Melt into the cave floor like a person built from snow.

Indeed, she felt like she had been born anew. As if she had died recently and was now a fresh creation scrubbing the dead from her body, water dripping off of her like tears.

When Simone was finally done, she spread her large blanket out on the floor in front of the fire, padding around softly in her bare feet, making sure it didn't catch. Then she laid down and wrapped it around her.

The flames danced in her eyes as she lay there, using her balled up coat as a pillow. Hungry, sore, and still a little bit cold; Simone wondered about those back at the camp. Who had made it? She hadn't wanted to see but now she was curious. Perhaps the slaves had overtaken them when the gates had opened. Maybe, by some miracle, the slavers had set them free. Unlikely, but it felt good to think it possible. More than likely it had all happened as she had expected it to. The doors had been opened, the people inside had cowered and pushed together, and the barbarians had rushed in and bludgeoned them to death.

It hurt to think about, but before she could dwell on it for long Simone drifted off into a deep and dreamless sleep.

EARLIER THAT NIGHT, after Simone had climbed out of the snow, if she had walked the other way—the way back towards the camp—she would have seen. She would have discovered that the slaves had not lived—not risen up and taken over. That the cages had not even been opened. They had died.

Everyone had died.

As soon as the obsidian man's head had come apart, madness had begun to rise in the camp. Like a shockwave, it spread and grew and boiled. As Simone had laid there buried like a seed, every living man and woman eventually fell in and devoured each other as a seething mass of famine incarnate. Burning hot and bloody, every single one of them died screaming and were torn apart with the sounds of wet tearing and gnashing teeth. And if Simone had been there to see, her soul would have come apart like so many before her that have stared Hell in the face and been blinded to nothing but its blazing existence in the very fabric of the starving world.

9
———

JOSHUA

T he night was cold but lacked any real bite. The sun had been out that day more than usual and the dense atmosphere held the warmth like an old friend that had been lost to it for years. The comfort of the day had felt almost alien to Joshua, like the misleading quiet that preceded an attack. But the attack had never come.

The entire time Joshua traveled up into the hills he was careful to keep his ears open for voices. Voices meant multiple people, and multiple people usually meant bad people. Those who gathered in groups usually only did so for power, and while occasionally that power meant safety, like The Harbor settlement that laid to the South, the people with power typically used it to rob people of their property, freedom, or lives.

While it was true that slavery wasn't the lucrative, well-maintained industry it had been once, it was still brutal and terrifying. Perhaps even more so now that it had less structure. Joshua remembered learning about the transatlantic slave trade that had once ripped people from their homes and sent them so far away that, even if they did manage to escape, they never had any chance to return. He thought of the skeletons that must have littered the bottom of the

Atlantic and the frustration one had to have felt as they were pressed beneath the heels of—not just a group of heavily armed people like those that resided in The Valley—but an entire nation—an entire government and populace that felt neither hatred nor sympathy for you, but simply regarded you and your enslavement as a natural occurrence in nature—your freedom a ripe apple fresh for harvest.

Things were different now, but not all that much. One could say that people were more violent now than they had been back in those days and they'd be right. The violence that existed now was the constant struggle for survival, whereas their peace had been closer to the peace and quiet after a nuclear weapon has yielded its tonnage upon an unsuspecting population. Screams silenced before they could be uttered, tears evaporated before they could fall.

A lot of people here—even some of the slaves—considered everyone free and maintained that they had chosen slavery by not dying. There was no law here, so everyone was free to do whatever they wanted. And that freedom often yielded the same results of the nuclear weapons of ages past.

"The cost of freedom isn't just dead soldiers," Joshua's father used to say. "The cost of freedom is living with the free." And he would know better than most.

Four months before Joshua's sixteenth birthday, his father had been killed in a pedestrian crosswalk by a drunk driver. After multiple IA investigations, dash cams would show the man who had been driving had been pulled over three miles up the road before he was let off with an informal warning by his future brother-in-law: Sheriff's deputy Ronald Gill. He had then driven into town, and with his heart utterly devoid of murder, had still committed it.

"Manslaughter" was the official term, but Joshua had a hard time seeing it that way as a kid. It didn't matter what they called it. His father was still dead, and he had been killed by another man. To a 16-year-old there wasn't a single word in the human language that could capture what he felt.

Joshua never forgot the unspoken lesson of his father's death: grace never failed to yield its punishment. Deputy Gill had decided to turn the other way for someone who was soon to be the next closest thing to a blood-relative, and in doing so, the cost of the punishment was not cast upon either of the two men, but upon someone absent from the conversation entirely.

That lesson had stuck with him—had become as much a part of him as anything else his father had tried to teach him. Someone always paid.

The forest outside hummed and cackled with unidentifiable animal noises, but Joshua felt relatively secure in the cave he had found. It wasn't so much a cave as it was a tunnel that had been dug into the dirt and reinforced with freezing slush. It was a bizarre feature, but the reflective ice made the whole inside look like a mirror funhouse.

Before he could even settle down Joshua had built a fire quickly and with great anticipation. He still couldn't quite believe the fact that he had a box of working matches. How he had marveled and shook as he struck a single matchstick against the side of the box and watched the tiny flame flare and level out, scattering the creeping darkness. It was so wonderful that he had almost let it burn down to his glove, but right before it did he had dropped it into a small pile of shaved birch bark. Now that the fire danced in front of him the walls were made to look like great, wet distortions of reality. Light bent and made it look as if time had shifted and stopped, catching Joshua in a fossilizing amber, stretching and warped.

Tomorrow was going to be a long day regardless of how many people he ran into, and he didn't expect to see many. He still had to find the tributary. It had gotten dark faster than Joshua had expected it to and he had had to find shelter quickly. Somehow he had lost track of time. Slowed his pace. Something. So now he had to wake up before dawn tomorrow and set out to find the river. It wouldn't be hard, but it would be an extra step on what already promised to be a long day.

Joshua went over and grabbed a few dry sticks he had dragged in from outside to add to the fire. The snow that had been stuck to them now lay in a tiny puddle that had begun to trickle down and into the cave. The miniature streams pushed over small rises and accelerated through dips in the icy floor. He wondered absentmindedly how big the river was with all of its tributaries. A million tiny paths that wound in and out of each other, accumulating in lakes and getting tangled in nests of ponds that looked like small skirmishes in a quest for the ocean.

Sparks went up in the air as Joshua nudged the closest burning stick with his foot. The fire wouldn't last long. The sticks were too small and too few, and eventually, it would go out. Right then and there Joshua made a decision. He would try to rest now, and as soon as the fire went out, he would pack up and head out in search of the river. Darkness be-damned.

The canoe was tipped upside-down outside and covered in snow. He would roll up his blankets, hitch up the canoe, and begin his journey.

Joshua sat down up against the frozen wall, ghosts and embers dancing silently around him. He pulled the blanket up to his neck, made sure that his legs and feet were out of the trickle of water running down into the tiny tunnel, and clutched the handle of the hatchet he had been given by Wren. He inhaled. His throat was hoarse, his ribs still sore.

THE MURMUR of voices woke Joshua instantly.

He couldn't make out the words but they were close. The fire had died completely and too late he realized that it had not been a good idea. The night had been warm enough to sleep without one, he had just been so damn excited to use those matches.

Joshua dropped the blanket soundlessly off of him. The hatchet was heavy in his hand, but this wouldn't be the first time he'd had to use something like it to defend himself. He just hoped that the inter-lopers weren't armed any better.

Crawling on his hands and knees, he crept towards the mouth of the tunnel. The ground was wet. A thin layer had been melted by the heat of the fire and the slight decline into the ground made the whole floor slippery. If Joshua hadn't been thinking, he would have jumped up and rushed out to see who was there. His boots would have squeaked, his legs would have gone out from under him, something. He would have given his position, been drug out into the snow, and then been shackled and beaten. But he didn't. Instead, he stayed calm. Stayed quiet.

The voices were silent now but he could hear the distinct crunch of wet snow beneath heavy boots. They couldn't find the tunnel. Maybe he should just stay here. Let them pass. That had been his plan, hadn't it? If he saw anyone on the road he would stay low and avoid them.

This was different though. If they didn't find him they could still find the canoe, and that could absolutely not happen. The canoe was hidden, but not as well as it should have been, and that was Joshua's mistake. He should have taken the time. Maybe even drug it in with him.

He couldn't risk it catching fire though. Didn't have the energy to try and pull it around the little corner that obviously hadn't been enough to block the sight of the fire. Shit. He should have known better. As soon as he saw the way that the walls glowed and reflected the firelight he should have known that it would act as a giant fucking flashlight that anyone could see.

Blood surged through Joshua's veins. The cold leaked out through his feet and his body was filled by the warmth of anticipation. He had finally been able to move to a crouching position right at the mouth of the tunnel. He glanced back one more time to make sure that the fire was truly out—that no one could see it. They must have spotted it from a ridge somewhere. Lost sight of it quickly but continued to head in the same direction. They must know the land, be using land-marks to get so close without getting turned around.

How many were there? Joshua peered around the corner and looked out. The night was brighter than he had expected. The moon hung low and closer to the horizon than Joshua's internal clock said it should have. Shadows long and dominant, like great pools of ink upon the fleece-white snow.

There. A shifting figure. Joshua's eyes slowly began to pick apart silhouettes as they moved slowly through the woods. Four? Five? He glanced over at the canoe and blanched when he saw a curious face making a straight line towards it. He hadn't cried out yet. No hushed "over here," or "look what I found." He just drifted towards it like a wooden ship into uncharted waters. Slow but unstoppable.

That's when Joshua noticed the bat. Long and wooden and edged in unidentifiable pieces of sharp metal that only glinted in the moonlight as it rose with the young man's stride, and then descend back into shadow as it fell.

Joshua was confident now that he could not be seen. The top of the tunnel hung down and the moon was at an angle that cloaked the entire entrance in shadow. The canoe lay roughly five feet away, naked in the silver light. The others continued on, and Joshua realized that eventually, he would have to call out if he didn't want to be left behind.

The hatchet was not ideal in this situation. He would have to raise it and expose himself. Not to mention the canoe that he would have to hurdle over. It lay directly between them and Joshua had a feeling that the intruder would signal the others before walking around to the other side. A fantasy flashed through his mind where he threw the hatchet and it stuck into the man's forehead, the rigid body falling back silently into the snow with a slight gurgle. Impossible. He couldn't throw a hatchet with any accuracy, and even if he could he would have to be extremely lucky to kill the man with it. More than likely it would hit him in the face and break his nose. No, whatever he did would have to be fast and fool-proof. They'd make noise no matter what, but if the man was down quick enough he could be gone before anyone located him. Plus there was the canoe...

Maybe he could hide under it? Terrible idea. The first thing they would do after finding the body would be to flip the canoe over. Maybe he could hide the body under the canoe? Still no. If Joshua succeeded there would be too much blood. Impossible to hide in the snow.

He thought for a second as the young man moved in, and made up his mind. The hatchet, after all, wasn't the only weapon he had at his disposal.

THE MAN WAS WEARING a heavy fur coat and a scarf to cover his breath. His neck wasn't exposed but Joshua didn't think he'd have any trouble finding it. As soon as his target reached the canoe, glanced around, and focused in on the others in his party, Joshua leaped and in two big strides he covered the distance between him and the canoe, jumped over it, and plunged the hunting knife deep into the man's neck. He stabbed him three more times as they both fell to the ground, and then another seven, finally punctuating it with the wet smack of the hatchet Joshua held in his other hand.

From there he crouched down, kept low, and moved away with the hopes that the canoe would block their line of sight.

"*Jitter?*" He heard the man's questioning tone fraught with panic. Or maybe it had been "Ritter."

Joshua was already gone, looping back around. There were definitely four others that he could see. The largest, most threatening one was closest to where Joshua was now moving. Unfortunately, he was also the most alert. The snow, the heavy clothes, it all made too much noise on Joshua as he ran, and as soon as he was close enough to the big one, the man swung suddenly towards him and cried "hey!"

The element of surprise was lost. Joshua was used to avoiding threats, not engaging them. His body was always amped for a fight, and being the smart man he usually was, he tended to avoid these situations. It wasn't that he craved blood or death, it was something psychological, or maybe biological. He wasn't sure. All he knew was that he needed to avoid certain situations, and this was just the kind.

His target wielded what looked like some sort of stick, and though Joshua couldn't see it, he would have bet that it had some sort of sharp edge fastened to it. The man swung, and Joshua was proved correct. The dark, jagged stone that was embedded in the wood sliced through the left arm of Joshua's fur coat and then continued through his leather coat underneath and finally into the flesh of his upper arm. Thankfully the edge didn't stick out far enough to cut very deep, and was so inconsistently jagged that it snagged on the coat on its way out.

The big man was strong but not experienced enough to plan a second strike. Instead, his weapon got caught and he lost his grip on the handle. Joshua had all the time he needed to deliver a counter. He had picked up the dangerous-looking bat that his first victim had dropped, and was now drawing back for a swing.

The man was too shocked, too tired, lacked the kind of experience that he should have had if he had lived here long. Must have been fresh from beyond the mountains. Joshua swung the bat at his wide and milky eyes as if to send his entire head back to the land it had come from, but instead just managed to cave in his skull with a sickening crunch.

The other three were on him. They were spread far enough apart that Joshua thought he could take each of them if he was fast enough. He tried to pull the bat from the dead man's skull but it was stuck. The hatchet came back out of his belt along with the knife he had stuck hurriedly into his pocket, and as he withdrew it he felt fabric give way and made a tiny mental note not to try and store anything in the right side of his pants.

The first on-comer was a skinny man wielding a large knife. He halted as he reached Joshua, danced out of the way of a knife thrust, ducked to counter, but was slashed from above with the hatchet. The blade was aimed at his head, but the man was moving faster than anticipated, and the sharp metal cleaved a chunk out of the left side of his neck.

Blood jetted out over the snow in huge, arterial spurts.

The second one was short. *A kid maybe*, Joshua thought absent-mindedly. He bore nothing but a large rock that he hurled. Joshua didn't even need to dodge it.

The hatchet and knife felt like uneven claws from a mutant hand —both slick with blood and screaming for more. Joshua's muscles ached with desire. He felt like he was moving at quadruple speed—as if everything was already over: the kid's scared face; the grunt as the knife sunk into his gut; the final man's wail; running over with tears in his eyes; moving to cover his son from the monster that had invaded their land; trying to block the blow with his forearm; one, two, three hacks and his arm ended just below the elbow; the terrible, drunken, gore-soaked murder that followed.

AN HOUR and Forty-five minutes later and Joshua was unhitching the canoe's rope from around his waist at the river's edge. Breathing evenly through his nose, he stared down into the eyes of his reflection. Not only did he recognize himself, but felt as if he had for the very first time.

He had found the river but suddenly felt a strong urge to stay right where he was.

THAT MORNING the sun rose like blood to the surface of a smooth lake, but Joshua was already too far up the river and into the cave to see it. The current was weak here. On the nose of the canoe was the torch Wren had given him, and it sliced through the darkness of the cave like steel through flesh. The path was easy. Time sifted past like the water, each oar stroke sending it into a tailspin. The stakes weren't needed. Rest wasn't needed. He was beginning to think that he never needed either to begin with.

It didn't hit him right away, but Joshua slowly became aware of the smell of smoke. The sweet smell of cooking wood and vegetation. It swirled and grew and eventually Joshua's eyes were watering. He tried not to, but he couldn't help it: he coughed. Lightening branched through his chest. He hadn't felt the pain when he was exerting himself earlier, but the damage to his ribs was extremely evident now. He coughed over and over again. A rapid, hacking cough that couldn't get enough air to be deep and booming. His eyes were pouring, a bitter rain upon a coat so matted with blood that he must have looked like some poor creature turned inside out.

Despite the lack of oxygen, he rowed feebly forward.

Just when he thought he was going to die of smoke inhalation the air began to clear and an unsettling warm breeze swept underneath him. Through bleary eyes, he slowly perceived the world around him.

The atmosphere was a haze of smoke that was thrown around in the wind, obscuring sight in some places while revealing it in others. The air was hot and thick and the baser part of Joshua's brain screamed at the idea of such a massive blaze and told him that he should run. All around him the world burned. A charred landscape of perpetual immolation through which the river cut unscathed like a pardoned man through a crowd of the hopeless and damned.

He continued to row, his chest still heaving and burning. The river was still narrow but he could see behind him where it branched off into two sections: the one from which he had just emerged, and the one he had ridden down into The Valley so long ago.

The current was still unfathomably weak. In Joshua's experience, big rivers ran fast at their narrow points and slow at their wide ones. He didn't know too much about water flowage, but he figured it must have meant that this river was different from others, or that somewhere in the mountain it was fed by many other sources of water, each hailing from an unknown world.

Either way, it made him uneasy. He felt like some animal walking into a trap. Or not a trap per-say, but he perceived that the water beneath him did not rage against his ascent up the river, not because it didn't care, but because it didn't matter. The hand had already been dealt. He, of course, perceived it all too late.

The flaming tree fell like an executioner's sword and with a mighty, sparking blow it cleaved the canoe into two useless pieces, burned and smothered in a single instant.

Joshua plunged to the bottom of the river so fast he thought there was something pulling him down, and there was in a way. All of his extra clothing and gear accumulated into a firm handgrip for the undeniable grasp of gravity. It sucked him down to the bottom, and for the second time in recent memory, he was drowning. Drowning in blood and violence and the futility of a search for which this was the only answer. The old man had been right. He had found the way out of The Valley. He would find what he was looking for.

Hanging in the dull, icy current with arms stretched apart and hands open wide he thought about the boy he had killed that morning—thought of the look on his father's face. He thought of a lot of things. Every life he had taken—every life he had ruined. He thought about the action that had led him here—the stone pillar around which every consequence of his life had been wound, unraveled, and pressed together in a heaping mess of unknowable results and intertwining paths.

The river that coursed around him became the accumulation of all his tears. He let them go.

10

OVIN

The road to the valley was relatively empty, but they took no chances. They traveled at night, no radio contact, no lights but the moon and stars. No fires, no streets, no pissing and moaning.

There were ten of them not including the five dogs. Ovin lead the hunt, Raquel was his right hand, heavy weapons were handled by Britt and Gustav, dogs by Peter, recon by Wesley, comms by Flint, and finally fire support was Russ, Jacob, and Travis. The dogs' names were Trixie, Captain, Cookie, Loop, and Charm.

They packed light, slept poorly, and were making good time.

"So who are these guys again?" Russ had moved up alongside Ovin as they walked. The landscape transitioned in and out of sparse brush and light woods, the sun glaring down at them like a spotlight. The brown camouflage they wore made it easier to go undetected, and the lack of settlements made for a lack of people, but they still had Wesley scouting out the road ahead.

"The Pack? Some sort of kill squad. Cut peoples' heads off, drown 'em in barrels, that sorta thing."

"What makes you think they don't know we're coming?"

"They might." Ovin wasn't particularly fond of Russ yet and

harbored some pretty strong feelings about him being assigned to the group for a mission like this, but his hunters needed as much information as they could get to do their job well, and Ovin had no problem telling any of them everything he knew. "They've been pretty on top of things apparently. Hit a few of Cruz's squads early on. Made a pretty big fuckn' mess out of 'em."

"And he wants em...what?"

Ovin looked at the dogs that moved in a rough phalanx out ahead of them. He tilted his head in their direction. "Dog food."

An incredulous smile crept over Russ's face. "Serious? Like, we gun 'em down, and feed them to the dogs?"

"Sort of." Ovin pulled what looked like a black plastic box out of his pocket. "This might be a bit before your time, but this thing right here records video to cassette tape. Simple. Just record what you want, eject the tape, give it to a guy who knows a guy, thing eventually finds its way to the big fish, and suddenly the big fish is swimming in a pond of his own piss."

"Shit." Russ took a minute to compose himself. "That's pretty cold-blooded. So I take it he wants them to be taken...alive?"

"If possible, yes. And no, that's not cold-blooded. That's war. These assholes have had their hands in drug running, human trafficking, cutting fuckn' kids' hands off 'n shit. This is nothing. This is the brightest, gentlest corner of the hell we're about to drop on these motherfuckers. This is retribution. Not to mention the fact that this was your old man's idea in the first place."

"Shit man, I guess," Russ said without sounding too convinced. "Yo, you got family? Something terrible happen to you or something to make you so, ya know, sick?"

"No, nothing terrible happened." Ovin had picked up his pace and he visibly saw Russ and a few others lean into their stride. "Parents are alive back home. No dead girlfriend. No best bud that OD'd on blow or anything. I'm just here to make a living and wipe a little bit of the scum away in the process."

"Trent said they took you in young. Your parents know you're here?"

Ovin was ready to give his people any pertinent information, but he was getting a little sick of all of the personal inquiries. "Yup, they know I'm here. No, they don't like it. And before you ask, no I don't have a gal I'm sweet on back home. I don't have some abusive high school mentor that pushed me into this. And if none of that is good enough for you, I'll show you some pictures some time of the shit these people do. If I'm looking for revenge for anyone, it's the families these guys soak in gasoline and light on fire. The moms and dads and aunts and uncles they torture to give up their loved ones. That's why I'm here. That's why I'm doing this. Now, how about you? I heard you're here because your daddy wants you to step on a land mine and get your fucking legs blown off. Make you spill some blood and paint yourself in it. Be the man he wished you had been from the start. So tell me, how you gonna do that? When we send him this video to give to his contacts, you gonna be behind the blood bath giving a thumbs up? Gonna see if you can score some kills and mail the fingers back to papa and hope he gives you the snuggles you deserved as a kid?"

The entire group came to a jarring halt as Ovin spun and faced Russ, and if he had been paying attention, he would have noticed the dogs begin to act differently. Their hackles raised and a low growling emanated from their throats. Somewhere far away, there was someone trying to get Ovin's attention.

"You try any of that? Any single *fucking* thing that puts this mission or these people in danger and I swear to God you'll be right alongside those barbaric motherfuckers getting the exact same treatment. So tell me asshole, why are you here? What's your plan? How are you going to *not* get mauled the fuck to *death* when we roll up on these dick heads?"

Russ was shocked to silence and looked almost on the verge of tears.

"Ovin." Wesley had come up on them but Ovin raised a finger for him to be silent.

Ovin gave Russ a hard look. "Next time you leave me hanging like you did back in that town, I will shoot you."

There were now tears in the boy's eyes. Wesley shifted uncomfortably.

"Got it?"

Russ didn't answer.

"Got it?" Ovin grabbed him by the coat and pulled him close.

"Yes," Russ sputtered.

"Say 'I got it.'"

Russ's lip quivered.

"Say it."

"I got it." Russ's voice was suddenly cold and unshaking. "I got it sir." There was no defiance. No docile submission. Ovin thought he saw something flit across Russ's face. Something dark and buried that burned low and constant. Something not meant for Ovin.

"Now." Ovin turned towards Wesley and noticed he was a bit more pale than usual. "What is it?"

"Something you should see," Wesley said in a low, shaking voice. His eyes were averted from Ovin's and when he was signaled to show them what he found, he turned and started back up the hill he had just run down, scoped rifle on his back.

They walked silently for a few minutes, and finally crested a hill that looked down on a small oasis. It felt like a long time before anyone said anything. Wesley lowered himself to a single knee and breathed out through his nose.

Ovin was the first to break the silence, and even then just barely.

"Jesus."

The word hung in the air as another name to add to the body count.

THE BODIES WERE SUSPENDED upon a crisscrossing net of wire. Some were strung through the flesh while others appeared to be tangled or fastened with other bits of metal. With the sun at its highest point, the bodies baked and bloated and acted as a beacon to the carrion birds that circled overhead like a black halo.

"What the fuck..." The utterance had been low and could have come from anyone, but Ovin recognized the hushed tone that Raquel often used and understood that she was deeply disturbed.

The metal wire wound and overlapped in places that made it look like a tangle of highways from the air, crossing paths rank with rot and coagulated blood.

"Why?" Peter, the dog handler, had Captain by the scruff of her neck and was trying to calm her down with a gentle hand. "The heads...I don't-"

"The Pack," Ovin said. "This is a message, for us, I think."

It had to be, for the bodies weren't just human bodies, they were also the bodies of dogs. Hairy and sagging, each dog had had its head removed and sewn onto the neck of a human, and in turn, each human's head had been placed on the body of a dog. The massacre seemed to hang in vivid motion like a wretched tableau, eyes wide and wet and screaming, man and animal alike.

"Those aren't soldiers or rebels up there," Russ said. "These are women. Children."

"You're right," Ovin said. "These are just townsfolk. This is a message, it's gotta be. But I don't know if it's referring to them, The Pack, or our own dogs." He looked down at Captain who was still trying to stand and pace.

"Should we cut 'em down," Russ asked.

Ovin thought for a second. "No. They're dead. They don't care what happens. And we can't spare the time or risk the danger of them being booby-trapped."

Russ nodded glumly.

"Just remember this-" Ovin turned towards the young man. "-when they're being ripped apart. Don't think about your dad or what he'll think about you." He pointed up at the nearest body, a girl, probably thirteen that had severe lacerations and bruises climbing up her naked body until they ended at the head of some mongrel breed, its lips snarled in rigamortis, teeth bared. "Think about what *she'll* think of you."

Russ's eyes were burning pits, with twin rivers streaming out of them.

THEY SLEPT on the ground in the naked sand that night, the dry air holding no moisture and no heat, the moon shining like a reflection of the sun on a frozen lake of impenetrable darkness.

"You think the kid'll be ok? You gave him a pretty hard time." Raquel's arms were wrapped around Ovin. Their relationship wasn't sexual, but it *was* physical. A warm touch and tenderness that both of them needed after days like today. They lay huddled together like orphaned siblings thrown clear of some past war.

"He needed it. What we saw today was-" Ovin thought for a second. "-Incomprehensible. But I hate to say it: it couldn't have come at a better time. I think he's going to use it. Wield it."

Raquel was quiet, her nose nestled into the back of Ovin's neck. He could tell she was thinking. She did more of that than talking, which is what made her valuable.

"Do you think we'll catch them?" Ovin asked. It was a question he wouldn't have asked any of the others under his command.

"I think we'll catch *up* to them," Raquel finally said. "I can't say how it'll turn out though."

Ovin nodded. The movement was so tiny that she only perceived it because she was so close.

They remained silent for the rest of the night and eventually drifted off to sleep. If they would have spoken about what they had dreamt about the next morning, they would have found that they shared the same dream: Huge, black wolves with amber eyes were stalking them; and when they bared their teeth the sharp incisors were silhouetted by a deep fire lit behind them.

But the two remained silent the next morning. They embarked on the last stretch of their journey before they hit a small town, and from there: the valley.

11

SIMONE

The hunt for her third victim was probably the easiest. He came to her. Simone didn't know how, but he must have known that Obsidian had died, because four days after she had fired the shot that put her one step closer to her final target, the next one, Red as she called him, had led a war party right into her camp. She hadn't been there of course. She had tuned in to the sounds of the forest pretty well in her time in The Valley. The squawks and chirps that typically accompanied the morning had faded away a full half-an-hour before she saw the first scout picking her way through the brush.

She was a thin woman with giant, bird eyes and she moved so quietly that the only reason Simone knew she was there was because she just so happened to be staring at the area she walked through.

Simone had learned how to move quietly in the forest, one slow step at a time, each one followed by watching, waiting, and listening. Sometimes it would take hours for her to move a hundred feet if the brush was dense enough. When she had seen the scout, she had just taken a step and had been observing, not just with her eyes but with her ears, her nose. Her gut.

She didn't know how she was going to take the woman down, and at this point, if she stayed absolutely still she didn't really see a reason to. Simone knew there were others behind her. Whenever she saw a bird in the air it was flying one way: away from the direction the scout had come. She also heard the furious chirping of rodents in the distance, the kind of chirping that they made when they saw something they viewed as a threat.

There was also a silence. It wasn't dead quiet, but the animal noises were different. No lively birdsong, no wrestling squirrels. Just the flapping of wings and skittering of feet and abbreviated warnings calls.

Even with all of these tiny signs adding up, Simone still could have written it off as some predator in the woods—she had seen things down here in The Valley that she hadn't seen anywhere else— she didn't think so though. She couldn't say what it was exactly. There was just this feeling of mounting pressure, like the buzz in the air before a storm. It was a tiny voice that was quiet but persistent, and Simone had learned to listen to it. To trust it.

How many? Ten? Fifty? There was no way tell. She just stood as still as she could as the woman crept by less than a hundred feet away. Simone wasn't as covered as she would have liked to be, and the rifle was slung over her back. She didn't think she could grab it in time, and even if she could, firing a shot would waste a precious bullet and practically do the scouts job for her. The .308 was *loud*, and firing it this close to the group would be nothing less than an auditory beacon.

So she waited. With eyes averted, so as not to engage the scout's sense of being observed, she stood as still as the trees around her. Even with ideal cover, she knew that motion would be her worst enemy.

The woman stopped suddenly. An inhaled breath stopped halfway down Simone's throat.

Like the earth on its axis, the woman's head turned arduously to her left, right towards the trees where Simone was hiding. The head stopped. Simone could feel eyes on her. Nothing moved.

Fifteen long heartbeats passed as the woman stared. Simone

knew what she was doing. The scout sensed something, felt that there was someone or something in the trees, but she couldn't see it. So she was waiting for movement.

Simone could only watch through her peripheral vision—eye contact would make discovery certain—but she thought she saw the woman's hand in her jacket. What did she have? A gun? A knife? She couldn't be certain, but she suddenly thought she knew. No, she *did* know. Call it intuition, but a few scattered pieces fell into place in Simone's mind. She had only seen it once and it had been a long time ago—a lifetime ago.

Memory flooded through her, and with it, pain.

They had been making breakfast, the girls were taking turns stirring flapjack batter while Avi, Simone's sister, cooked bacon in a cast-iron skillet. Simone remembered how Triggi, one of the twins, had been wary of the spitting grease from the bacon as she had been burned by it when it had popped and sprayed her arm a couple of weeks ago. There had been no burn marks or lasting damage, she had just been frightened by the sudden pain, and now kept her distance.

Simone had remembered wondering as she swept the floor that morning if Triggi would ever willingly go near a cooking pot again.

She wouldn't.

The deep boom had rolled through the hills like a death toll.

Noah, the owner of the ranch, had gone out to see if he could hire a few extra hands. He had become a surrogate father to the girls, and despite the multiple risks he had taken in virtually adopting an entire family, business was increasing along with his need for skilled workers. Noah owned a sizable chunk of property; treated his workers like family; and upon hearing of Avi's pregnancy, made every effort to accommodate her.

Simone felt a deep pang in her gut when she heard the explosion. There was nothing definitive that told her it was Noah that had just been ripped from the world of the living, that is if anyone had even died at all. But somehow, as if she caught a glimpse of the future ahead of her, Simone knew she would never see him again.

Avi had been pushing for Simone to find a husband. Have children. It might be a while, but eventually, they wouldn't have to hire anyone to help, they could keep it all in the family.

The farm they lived on wasn't a typical farm by any means, but a Reindeer farm. Up in Alaska, Reindeer were far more suited to the climate than most other herd animals and with the right amount of help, determination, and luck one could make a decent living.

Simone had grown up with Avi and two other sisters on a cattle ranch in Wyoming, but as they got older their family began to lose livestock to wolves that had been reintroduced to areas in the North. The numbers they would take were small at first—a few calves would turn up dead and mangled or maybe a lone heifer—but as time went on they started losing more and more. The pack around them steadily grew in number and Simone's family began to lose horses and dogs as well.

She had mixed feelings about the whole thing. On one hand, she hated to see everything she had seen her parents work for over the years destroyed. Simone had grown up watching her mother and father pour their lives into the ranch and then suddenly had to watch as it was whittled away. She hated it, and she hated that there was nothing she could do about it. The DNR offered help in these kinds of situations but proving that wolves were the culprits wasn't always as easy as it sounded. Sometimes a calf would just disappear without a trace, and no body meant no proof. Other times the wolves would circle the animals constantly, and a few of them would simply drop dead from the constant stress and adrenaline being poured into their systems. All in all, the wolf pack took far more animals than could be proven.

But Simone also knew that this was simply a pendulum swing from actions in the past. There was a time when wolves had been completely eradicated from the state of Wyoming, so once they had been reintroduced they had to reestablish themselves on the food chain. The fact that they had been pushed so close to the point of extinction was the very reason her family now had very little legal recourse when it came to protecting their property. She had come to

learn that that was simply how the bad in the world worked. Atrocities committed centuries ago were still wreaking havoc in the world
today. As one of the few African-Americans that was immersed in the
ranching lifestyle in the United States, she felt as if she understood
this greater than some of her peers. Then again, there wasn't a single
person she knew that wasn't reaping the devastating rewards of some
sin committed before they were born.

Even so, one day she had walked out to the herd and discovered a
calf laying on the ground with its back legs broken and its entrails
hanging out. It was still alive and trying to drag itself back to its
family, so Simone had run back to the house with tears in her eyes
and retrieved her rifle. With the barrel pressed up against the side of
the calf's chest, right where its heart would be, she mashed her eyes
shut and pulled the trigger. Then she grabbed it by its front legs, drug
it to the edge of the woods, and buried it. She didn't tell anyone, not
even Avi.

That night, after all of her daily chores were done, she told her
parents that she was going to go down to the river that ran along their
property and do some target shooting, which was technically true.
Although, she didn't tell them that she was bringing one of the huge
steaks from the big freezer in the shed.

Young and wrought with grief, she laid the big piece of red meat
out on a stump by the river bank and walked about 30 feet downstream where she laid down in the prone position. She waited for two
hours before she saw anything, then, just as dusk began to roll in, she
caught movement in the woods just beyond where she had laid the
steak. Slowly, a sickly looking dog-like creature padded wearily out of
the woods. It looked around briefly, and then made for the glistening
piece of flesh that must have smelled ever-so-inviting in the cool,
evening air.

Simone fired.

Within minutes she was standing over the twitching corpse. The
animal had fallen and writhed on the ground for a few seconds until
its movement began to slow and it became still. Simone stared down
at the wretched creature and would later remember thinking how

small it looked up close. It didn't look like the big majestic creature she had seen on TV, but more like what she imagined a german shepherd would look like if it lived in the woods its whole life, mangy and beaten.

Unceremoniously, she dragged it to the river, tossed it in, and walked back home.

It wasn't until about three months later when she saw a picture in a sporting magazine that she realized it hadn't actually been a wolf at all, but a coyote. Most of the coyotes had recently been driven out by their larger competitors, but for whatever reason, this one had stayed only to starve and grow sick. Simone tried to tell herself that she had done a good thing by putting it out of its misery, but for some reason, the memory had tasted bitter in her mind ever since.

Eventually, Simone's parents sold the ranch to open a butcher shop in Whitefish, Montana. Simone left for college, but two years later she took some time off to work as a ranch-hand in Northern Wyoming so she could afford her tuition.

That's when Avi got pregnant.

Avi had moved to Alaska, a place that ironically had a much larger wolf population than Wyoming. The difference was that they had been there for centuries and had long-established boundaries with the people who also lived there. Sure, a few animals would fall prey to them once and a while, but the instinct to avoid people was far greater than in a land they were new to.

Noah Harkness had been looking for help on the farm; and seeking a change in scenery, Avi had gone North. She helped to make sure that the animals were counted, fed, herded, and generally looked after. The reindeer were a bit less docile than the cattle she had grown up around, but their demeanor seemed to fit the wild landscape better, and once Avi had acclimated to that she had few problems acclimating to the work at hand.

Triggi and Gail had been born on a cold February night, to a mother who loved them, and a father who knew nothing of them and never would. Avi had met a man in town the previous spring and had spent one feverish night with him in her cramped apartment. He had bought her a drink, they got to talking, and by the time the sun was cresting the horizon the place where he had lain was already cold. He had been a traveling musician. A local bar in town had live music every Friday night, and looking to let her hair down a bit, Avi had joined a few of her co-workers for a bit of drinking and dancing.

Simone had joined her a few weeks after Avi had called her crying on the phone. Through gasps and sobs, she had lamented how she would probably have to take time off of work and how disappointed Noah would be in her.

"What does he care?" Simone had said. "Your personal life isn't his business."

But Avi had explained how he couldn't afford to lose her for even a few weeks. She could have taken a leave of absence, but without pay, she had no way of supporting herself.

"What kind of business doesn't have maternity leave these days?" Simone said rolling her eyes.

"He runs a pretty small operation." Avi had started sounding a bit defensive. "It's less than 20 people, and even so, he *does* offer it. I just don't think he can *afford* it is all."

"Well, if he can't afford it maybe he shouldn't be in business in the first place."

The line was quiet for an uncomfortable second. Then finally Avi said, "Look I didn't call to argue, I'm just looking for advice." Her voice was cold.

Simone apologized. They hung up after talking for a few more minutes, and three days later Simone had made her decision. She would stand in for Avi for the daily duties, and the two of them would live off of the single wage. It wasn't legal per-say, but Noah was relatively easy to convince. He offered to pay the maternity leave of course, but Avi wouldn't have it, so instead, he used his spare time to build a small house next to the main farmhouse and let Avi sleep in his guest room during its construction. Simone had some money saved up, so she quietly lived in and finished out the lease on her sister's studio apartment in town.

It was hard not to resent Avi for putting Simone in this situation.

Granted, it had been Simone's idea to go North to help her out, but even so, there was a little piece of bitterness in her that she failed to get rid of. Simone was silent and hardworking, but she was also stubborn. She had a hard time letting things go even if she knew they were wrong to hold on to.

"What were you thinking?" she had finally asked her sister one night. "It's not like they don't sell condoms *everywhere*."

"Oh, I guess it's hard to explain," Avi said dreamily. "It was like being overcome by this *fever*, ya know? It's like birth control wasn't even an option—like it was some foreign idea in a different language that I had absolutely no way of knowing about. Of course, I *did* know about it, but at the time it just never occurred to me. I mean, you can't think about something if you're not thinking about it, ya know?"

Simone didn't know. Sometimes Avi could be so careless. In fact, one could even say that it was one of her finest qualities. For instance: Simone never heard a single bad word about the guy who had knocked her up and left. Her sister simply took it for what it was and moved on.

Personally, Simone couldn't even imagine bringing some stranger home with her. She knew it was abnormal, but never in her life had she felt that sort of attraction for a man, or for a woman for that matter. She had walked in on people having sex before or heard them through thin walls, and it all just seemed so messy and rough. Simone saw no difference between the way people did it and animals. She had tried a few times but just never got it. Despite not being able to secure a husband and have children to help out on the farm, it didn't bother her in the least. In fact, most of the time sex only seemed to make things more complicated, so she was perfectly happy to have nothing to do with it.

She loved those girls though—she wasn't a mother, but what she felt for them couldn't be any less than what Avi felt. Simone felt almost *responsible* for them. Not like they wouldn't exist without her, but she was certainly tied to their future. It didn't happen all at once, but over time she came to the conclusion that she would give anything for them.

Even her freedom.

They heard the distant boom that morning and knew that someone would not be coming home to their family. It could have been anything really—someone illegally fishing with dynamite, the DNR destroying a beaver dam—but something about the sound carried with it a sort of grim foreboding, almost as if the most sensitive part of their brains perceived the slight variation between an explosion that tears through wood and earth and an explosion that tears through flesh.

There had been rumors circulating. A large group of unknown individuals had been making their way through the countryside. Some suspected a new backwoods militia, while others thought it might be a group of terrorists. All that was known for sure was that before they came—before people were murdered or stolen—there was a boom.

Simone later learned that they had come from what some people called "The Valley." It had a virtually mythic history with both the indigenous and non-indigenous people in the area. It was said that people disappeared around there. Over the years a countless number of planes and hiking groups had been lost. Police and other official investigative groups would follow the trail of the missing, but once inside the trail would go dead. Noah had said one evening that over the last few years the people around there had started to become restless. Too many people had been lost. Too many questions had gone unanswered. It was just a matter of time before people began to organize.

But it hadn't happened yet. The incidents were too infrequent, the information too scarce. For now, people just stayed on their guard. For all the good it did them.

Simone remembered how Avi had spun wide-eyed towards the window. An anxious moment passed before they were all clamoring towards the cellar.

Simone stood still as death, knowing what was under the scout's coat. It had taken a while to connect the dots, but once when she was a little girl her family had gone to watch one of the neighboring farms use dynamite to loosen up the soil for a new field. The explosives were good for dislodging boulders and tree stumps, and while there were other ways of accomplishing the task, the man who had owned the farm said there wasn't anything that got the job done quite like "old-fashioned TNT." Simone remembered the thick and reverberating sound it made when it went off, and she instinctively knew that, somehow, the woman standing just a stone's throw away, had some means of detonating herself as her neighbors had of detonating the fields in which they had later grown their food and livelihood.

An image came to Simone's mind of the woman wrapping her arms around her like some long lost family, and then their bodies would scatter apart like sand in the wind, sending up a signal to the others that at least one had died, and if there were others, they lay in this direction.

The scout stalked birdlike among the trees. She hadn't seen Simone, nor would she. She pecked forward with her quiet payload tucked firmly against her chest, ready to take flight at any moment. Simone would see that she did.

The plan worked almost perfectly at first. Simone moved quickly and quietly away from the scout, ducking and winding her way through the woods, and as soon as she felt she had gone far enough she began to loop around. The trees provided good cover and she was far enough away that a little movement and noise wouldn't be too much of a problem as long as she didn't run into anyone else.

She didn't. Simone made it to a bluff just ten minutes ahead of the woman, and by the time she saw her twig-like form slink into view her breathing had steadied and her heart rate slowed.

She shouldn't be doing this. What she was about to do was both dangerous, and if she thought really hard about it, unnecessary. Simone had an inclination towards the unnecessary though. She knew that she could move past the group, get behind them, stalk them from a distance, and pick off Red at her leisure. An opportunity would always present itself if one had the patience.

She also knew however that the scout would live. The same kind of person that would give her life so that others may gain the advantage in the enslavement and murder of people like Avi. Like the girls. She knew that she was the same kind of person who had pointed them out to the four leaders and explained that they were slowing them down on their way back to The Valley—that they would have to give up the women and children if they were to make it back before the authorities caught up to them. The men were the valuable ones. Never mind that Simone had worked a farm her whole life. They couldn't test the physicality of each and every slave to determine their worth. So that's why the women and children were lined up along the river bank facing the cool, running water and listening to gentle bird-song as the Pale Man had caved in each of their skulls with a heavy stone.

His work had been fast but not thorough, or Simone wouldn't still be breathing. Passed over by death, she had dug the grave and piled the bodies, and then endured an eternity of mourning. And in that eternity, where there existed the lifeless bodies of the closest thing she had to a real family, there would also exist her wrath. It would be an unquenchable flame that struck men blind with its very fury and pulled the Heaven into Hell so as to evaporate the both of them in a hiss of boiling steam and screaming souls.

As she stood there and thought about it, Simone didn't want to kill the scout. Or to kill the other men who had wrecked her life so totally.

She wanted to kill everyone.

Not far away, the man with the red beard cracked his knuckles. He knew the one who had killed his brother was close, but in actuality, he didn't much care. An opposing war party that had begun amassing to the North was on track to hit the main camp within a few day's time, which was something Red didn't want to miss. It was all he lived for in fact. The planning, fevered pitch of battle: it was who he was. After all, it had been *him* who had planted the seeds for the war party in the first place. He had whispered and turned the hearts of so many outside of The Valley that they would soon come pouring in to seek their vengeance. Nothing would slag their thirst for it, and by the time they were defeated there would be that many more slaves in The Valley.

No, the other one was just a minor player. She had followed just like the others and in doing so she was bound here for the foreseeable future. If they came across her then great, but the main objective was to leave a big enough trail back to the camp where the Pale Man now resided. That was the real goal here.

And at that moment, a distant boom rolled over the hills.

On second thought, Red mused, *maybe today has a little more fun to offer than I had originally expected.*

12

SIMONE

Simone watched a massive group of armed men and women enter a clearing from the edge of the bluff she was perched on. It wasn't the bluff that currently had the scorch marks of dynamite against its face or a fractured corpse at the bottom of it but an adjacent one that overlooked the one she had just left; it also overlooked the woods below and the clearing just beyond.

They carried spears and knives and hatchets and clubs. If Simone had observed Red long enough—how he moved and planned—she would have known these frothing killers for what they were: cannon fodder.

But she didn't, and to her, they were all just kindling for the fire. They would all die sooner or later.

Simone had expected them to run straight at the place she had been. They would have had to, right? What good was a signal if you couldn't follow it? But as she looked down at the clearing she observed a group of her pursuers fan out. Could they know? Should she move? No way they would dig this far into the brush on the side of a bluff right?

She wasn't so sure now.

It was a long shot--maybe 700 meters--but she thought she could make it. A professional shooter could have done it easily, but that's not what she was. She was a natural, there was no doubt about that, but she had no actual formal training. Back in Wyoming, she had spent hours at dusk seeing how many sticks she could knock down. She had to start out with big pieces of birch bark with a circle etched into the middle so she had reference points on whether she was pulling to the left or aiming too high, but eventually she moved to just jamming sticks in the ground and shooting them in half. She would zero in on the tiny knots and send splinters spiraling away in a cracking explosion. As she got better she moved the sticks further and further out, started practicing in the wind and the rain and began to learn to account for airspeed and density—learned to adjust for bullet-drop. Eventually, she could do it without thinking. Her senses would log the information automatically, and when she lifted the rifle she knew instinctively where the bullet would go.

To an extent at least.

Simone knew she could hit a man at 700 meters, but she wasn't sure if she would kill him. She stood a pretty good chance of course. Getting hit by one of the .308 rounds was like being punched by a train. When she had killed the coyote back home as a teenager, she had seen how it left a tiny hole in the entry point and a massive, gaping wound on the other side. She learned that bullets "mushroom" when they hit their target and the force of the impact expands outward as it exits.

Most likely, Red would have a chunk of his lung torn out or a major vein would be severed and he would bleed to death.

Simone couldn't afford "most likely" though. She had two rounds left and she needed him *dead*. And she wasn't going to start on the others until she saw him go down and stay there. Her plan for the others was quickly changing though. She now had an unexpected payload of firepower on her, but when she saw the soldiers spilling out into the clearing her mind began to backtrack quickly. She had expected fifteen, twenty at most. What she saw in that clearing though had to be closer to two hundred. How could someone feed an army like that? What did they live on?

Simone needed Red to show his face right now so she could drop a slug directly into his chest and then she could leave the rest of them dazed and confused.

C'mon. C'mon.

Her heart was beginning to beat fast in her chest. Any moment she expected someone to burst out of the trees behind her and skewer her into the ground.

Somewhere behind her—not close, but closer than she would have liked—she heard voices. They weren't trying to be quiet in their approach, so they must have been trying to drive her somewhere. That or they were extremely confident in their pursuit and simply didn't care.

There.

Right at the edge of the clearing, a large man with a huge, red beard emerged from the woods holding a massive spear. His countenance was strong and confident and as soon as she saw him her body took over and raked the sight over his distant image and adjusted and fired. The boom seemed even louder than the dynamite had, but he never heard it. She watched the round hit him square in the chest and in seconds he was on the ground, his body slowly sinking into the snow as the blood rushed out of his smashed heart and melted a pathway back to the earth beneath him.

Simone was up and running, her legs felt like they were made of feathers and if she were to jump off of the bluff alongside her she thought she could maybe swoop down into The Valley and fly onwards towards the grey ocean that lay thin and stretched at the edge of the horizon. She bounded over logs and around trees and bushes, all the while thinking about her kill.

Another down. Only one more to go. One more to go. She didn't even care about the others now. She had planned on staying with them, picking them off one by one until they were all gone but now she realized what a folly that was. Even if she moved with stealth and precision, there was no way she would be able to kill that many without being hunted down and captured eventually.

Her head was buzzing.

The man slumped over and over in her mind. She played it again and again. The shock, the body going rigid and then limp in less than half of a second. Face fucking down. Like Avi. Like the girls. The image of his crumpled body was a soft butterfly in her heart, stroking and fluttering.

The body slumping against the fence, the rope around his neck. She saw him, saw Red—his eyes—she saw him give up.

The image hit her like a club and she almost fell. Why would she think that? Red and that boy were nothing alike. One was the victim, and the other the perpetrator. That kid was hanging there because of people like Red. *Red* deserved to be in that noose, not the boy.

Suddenly she wanted nothing more for than him to be alive again. She wanted to do it differently. A bullet was too quick. She saw that now.

Dammit. Dammit. Dammit.

She would have raised him from the dead if it meant being able to kill him again. Make him die a worse death. A thousand worse deaths, over and over again. All four of them lined up and being lowered slowly to the ground with a noose around their neck. And as she thought about the four of them flopping mute and terrified, her stomach turned with the memory of the kid. Two feelings warred inside her, vengeance and sadness. Both fed the other and the world suddenly tilted on its axis.

She stopped, the ground spinning underneath her. She reached out and grabbed a tree for balance. The small amount of food she had eaten that morning came up in a wash of stomach acid, chased by an onslaught of dry heaves. Somewhere in the back of her mind, she registered the feeling of running footsteps pounding the ground nearby, and when she looked up through teary eyes she observed in shocked terror that her prayer had been answered.

Figures stood all around her, and right out in front of them was the man she had just killed, his hair as fiery as Simone's gut. He smiled. The spears the other men carried made them look like giant, misshapen teeth; and the teeth closed in on her like a grinning jaw.

The explosion hadn't been loud, but it had been unmistakable. A few days ago a messenger had failed to show up and report the condition of Obsidian's camp, but Red had known before then. Just as he had known that Boils had died before that. Red could feel it—could feel his blood-brothers dropping, the only four who weren't—and who's disciples weren't—restricted to The Valley, or the ocean, or beyond. They were the necessary instruments that carved their way through every realm and fantasy—through every dream and nightmare, and those that survived were enslaved to them and those that died were not.

Red's soldiers raged around him like a sea of fangs, their bloodlust absolutely unquenchable. They had heard the explosion as well and had turned to him with eager questioning faces. The smallest of nods and they were off, pouring like angry fire ants up the hill. Most of them at least. He kept a handy few by his side, like his doppelgänger for instance.

He hadn't seen Obsidian's body, but he had seen Boil's, and he knew that whoever was hunting them killed from a distance. It was unlikely that she had survived the explosion, but it wasn't in his nature to make assumptions, only calculations. He had to weigh the odds and observe the pros and cons of every decision.

He knew his caution had paid off as soon as he saw the man who looked like him drop to the ground. And now, as he looked down at the woman bound and gagged before him, he reveled in the victory.

"Shouldn't we kill her?" one of Red's men asked him. He was a lanky man who was surprisingly adept with a spear. Even so, he lacked imagination.

"Of course not," Red said. "After all, what good am I-" and a big smile creased his face "-if I can't even enjoy my own spoils?"

13

JOSHUA

Trees swayed in the gentle wind that moved over the earth like a herd of peaceful spirits. They creaked lightly, soft music from times gone by. Joshua knew where he was. He was driving down the forest road on the way to his cabin. A bright and beautiful day abounded in all directions, and he had decided that a short nap on the rocky beach was what he needed right now. He'd lay out the folding chair with the reclining backrest right where the scraggly lawn ended and the water-washed rocks began.

It wasn't that it was quiet—quite the opposite actually—it was the noise that made it perfect. The sounds of the ocean were so bountiful that he could lay there and listen to them for hours, days, years. Even the huge storms that swept in and shook the walls of the small, wooden cottage and pounded its windows with huge wet fists were comforting. It gave him a sense of how small he was, and he took comfort in that. Certainties were hard to come by, but at least he knew his place in the world. Down here, on the spinning rock, the harsh sounds of a roiling storm didn't just offer clarity, they offered...*perspective.*

A few hours would be sufficient today. Just enough time to decompress before going back home to Julia. How wonderful she was. She gave him space he didn't ask for but often required, gave advice that he didn't know he needed, gave—she just *gave*. She gave of herself like no one he had ever seen. At first, it made him feel guilty, but then it had created a yearning in him, a desire to be *better*. Their friends always laughed at how out of his league she was, and they were right, he didn't deserve her and he never would. The fact was that it wasn't about him, it was about her.

With all of the windows rolled down, Joshua inhaled the rich aroma of fall as he drove slowly down the road that led to the ocean. Glancing at the rearview mirror he glimpsed his son in the backseat. His face was smooth and warm like his mother's, but his eyes were unmistakably his father's. They were like looking into a cool, crystalline, mountain lake; deep and clear enough to see the whole world. Joshua wished Julia was there with them, but she had had a funeral to attend, so it was just the two of them.

A station wagon trundled along the road behind them, and nonchalantly, Joshua wondered if they too had a cabin all the way out here.

Joshua could see his son looking out the window at the trees that moved steadily by. A wondrous place, to be sure.

Salt water sprayed up and into Joshua's face. He sputtered and tried to rise but strong hands held him down. There were trees around him; big, grey ones that heaved and creaked violently. Then there was the face. The sky was a man's withered face. The giant, tangled beard and searching blue eyes stared down like a painting of curiosity framed by naked, shaking trees.

"My God." His voice was rough and scratchy as if he hadn't used it for a long time. The trees weren't trees at all, but long, wet, matted chunks of grey hair that hung from the old man's head.

"Where-" a seizure of coughing gripped Joshua and he lay gasping for several seconds. "Where am I? The river—it—how did you find me?"

"The river?" The old man's face was questioning now. "We pulled you out of the *ocean*."

Joshua replayed the words in his mind. His head lulled and he squeezed his eyes shut. *The ocean?* He was thirty *miles* from the ocean. "Where-" He tried to get up and the man helped him with a gentle hand. "What is this?"

The man simply stared at him. He was soaked head to toe, was breathing hard, and stared disbelievingly up at Joshua. He blinked slowly and got to his feet. "How are you alive?"

"I don't know," Joshua said. "I think-" he squeezed his eyes shut again. He had been in the river—had been drowning. A thought struck him and he swayed. A *dream*? Was this a dream? Did he *imagine* his trek upstream? Wren? The boy and his son? All of it? He looked down to check his clothes but realized he wasn't wearing any. He had a large fur blanket wrapped around him and he was suddenly freezing. He tried to speak, but his teeth were chattering too loud and all he could manage was a shattered humming sound.

"Let's get you inside." The man finally said.

As they walked down the path towards a small building—both of their teeth chattering now—Joshua slowly recognized the place.

And his heart sunk.

He was at The Harbor, a small settlement located along the edge of the ocean just south of the river mouth. The ocean crashed and sprayed against the shore and Joshua now saw that he had been sitting on a dock. Did the old man pull him out of the water? How far out had he been? Since when do people save others down in The Valley?

He had somehow traversed the entire valley by water. Or had he? He still couldn't be sure what was real and what wasn't. His wet feet smacked on the stone that had been cleared of snow and ice, but he could still barely feel the contact of his skin on the rock. In fact, he was beginning to lose feeling in everything. He needed to get inside fast.

Or what? The voice in his mind was tired, exhausted. What would happen if he froze to death right here on the shore? Would he simply wake up somewhere else, not knowing how he got there? He wheezed out a cough.

"C'mon," the old man said. "We're almost there."

What a sight they must have been: two bearded, grey-haired, soaked-to-the-bone figures that stumbled through the doors of the common room and over to the fire like a pair of bedraggled dogs in search of shelter. Granted, Joshua was younger than his companion by at least a few decades, but old is old, and he felt it in his soul.

As they were warming up they were greeted with a few hesitant glances. The room was quiet but warm, and all-around sat men and women of all shapes, sizes, and ethnicities. Joshua had been to The Harbor before, but always avoided the bar, or "common room" as some called it. In actuality, there was a wooden sign over a counter stating the place's actual name: "The Way Side."

A few silent seconds passed. "They call this place the 'The Way Side?'" Joshua asked.

The old man pulled in closer to the fire. "One's who go here do. Others just call it 'shit-hole.'" Joshua saw his eyes dart over to him and back.

Suddenly, a hard-looking woman stalked over to them and threw a pile of clothes on the ground. "If they're too big you'll just have to get fatter." Her voice was raspy as if she had spent her whole life yelling. The old man gave her a small wave of thanks.

"That's Krissy, the bartender's her husband; she goes around and makes sure no one's killing each other."

"Sounds like a big job," Joshua said flatly.

"In here, I mean. Your life is in your own hands when you walk out those doors."

"You mean this place is some sort of...sanctuary?" The words were uncomfortable in Joshua's mouth, as if he were a full-grown man asking someone as to the whereabouts of Santa Clause.

The man tilted his head to the left and then back again. "That's a strong word. More like, a loose agreement. There's no dancn' or singn' or fuckn' speed-dating or anything."

"No alcohol then I presume?"

The man barked a laugh. "We got water here. Some fish for sale, that's about it."

"Mmmm." Joshua was warming up but he didn't feel like trying to put his clothes on just yet. The big blanket wrapped around him was thick and comforting. "So what do they call you?"

The man gave him a long, hard, searching look. People didn't much like being identified in The Valley, not that you could tell most of them apart; everyone was some combination of beaten, bearded, or broken down. No class clowns that was for sure.

Joshua raised a hand and closed his eyes. "No worries."

"They call me 'Gerald,'" he said finally. "Like the big boat that sunk? Same thing happened to me. 'Cept my boat was a small wooden fella and it sunk about fifty feet from shore. Almost took me right to the bottom, but I fought like hell. Boat's worth more to me than anything. Managed to drag it in eventually."

"Must have been a small boat."

"Sure is. Does me fine though."

Joshua threw off the blanket and leaned back to fumble through the pile of clothes. "Actually Gerald-" he picked out a pair of cloth pants that looked like they might fit. "It sounds like it doesn't."

Gerald sat there rocking gently, his eyes fixed on the fire like Joshua's son had fixed his on the passing trees so many years ago. The word "wondrous" floated into Joshua's mind and he felt a flutter of pain.

"Why's that boat mean so much to you?" Joshua was stepping into the legs of the pants. "Not like that ocean is particularly—uh—*accommodating.*"

Gerald just kept staring wordlessly into the fire.

"It's 'cause he wants to cross it," said a voice from behind.

Joshua turned around and observed a short robust man he thought he had seen before. The top of his head was shaved and his face was obscured by a massive beard on the left and a huge scar on the right. The man was a haunting portrait of someone who may have half-occupied the land of the dead.

"Drew." The man reached out and shook Joshua's hand before he could pull it away. "And before you ask, it's from a dog." He glanced around the room. "A fucking *big* one."

It would have to be, Joshua thought. It looked less like a bite from a dog than it did from a volcano. Huge streaks ran the width of his face, looking like the legs of some monstrous parasite attached to the side of his head. His voice was high and somewhat hoarse. Joshua figured that he must have damaged his larynx in the attack as well.

"Don't mind me saying, Drew, but you're a bit...*peppier* than the sort I'm used to." The same could be said of Joshua's own actions in the last few hours he realized. He typically kept to himself, avoided the crowd. And now here he was talking with two men in a crowded room that he had once simply called "shit-hole."

The man chuckled and Joshua saw it again, something familiar. He scrutinized his face. Drew was a good-deal younger than himself but even as he tried to picture his face without the beard and burns he couldn't place it. He stepped over to the pile of clothes and started rummaging through them for a shirt.

"Ya know," Drew said, "I couldn't blame anyone for thinking that. Most folk around here tend to be a little more like Gerry over there or yourself. Probably something to do with all the—ya know—*horror*." He smiled and Joshua had a thought.

"You know a man named Wren?" Joshua pulled a worn long-sleeve shirt over his chest and began looking for another.

Drew tilted his head in question.

"Lives up the river." Joshua gestured vaguely backward. "Ridiculous house. Fishes trash out of the water." As he was talking Joshua perceived the smallest amount of unease pass over Drew's face.

"Wren." He seemed to roll the word around in his mouth. "Yeah, I think so."

"You just sorta—*remind* me of him."

A cynical grin flashed on the scarred side of Drew's face. "Don't know if I should take that as a compliment or not, so I'll just forget it. Tell ya what, how 'bout we leave Gerry alone and we go sit down at a table over there."

Joshua dug some mismatched socks out of the pile of clothes, grabbed another shirt that was too big for him but would fit nicely over what he already had, and then he motioned for the pair of them to walk away from the fireplace, and for an instant, he was regretful of leaving the warmth. The new clothes suited him though, even if they smelled a little musty. As Joshua slid onto a wooden bench in front of a table he was surprised at how comfortable he felt. There was an assurance in this place. Not safety, just common interest.

"So..." Drew looked questioningly at Joshua and after a confused minute, he perceived the question.

"Joshua," he answered.

"Yes, Joshua, what brings you here?"

"Honestly, I'm not sure."

"How do you mean?" Drew gestured toward a man at the bar.

Joshua took a second to collect himself. "I've been looking for a way out of here—out of The Valley." He told him about Wren, about the river, about how he thought he had drowned but had then woken up here. He left out the old man he had killed—left out the wolves and the pile of bodies. Left out the people he had run into before rowing up the river. When he finished Drew gave him a long searching look.

All humor now gone from his face, he asked, "What are you looking for?"

"A way out," Joshua repeated.

"A way out...and?" Drew watched him.

"Answers."

The air in the room seemed to be dry and stale, as if it held the hanging dust of a race long-dead but unable to sleep. Ragged figures crouched over scraps of nothing, huddling for warmth and dreaming of escape. This wasn't a sanctuary or some step-up from where Joshua had been. He was in the exact same place, and he had yet to accomplish a single damn thing.

"And-" The next words were low, almost like a confession, and with them, he felt the shame of how he had given up on his reason for even coming to The Valley in the first place. "I'm looking...for my son."

14

JOSHUA

Joshua had stayed in a lot of hotels in his life. Some were crummy, some were luxurious, but never had he stayed in one in which he was unable to sleep. The Way Side was a different matter entirely.

There were rooms attached to the building but none were heated. The only two spaces that retained any heat whatsoever were the kitchen and the area in the commons that was closest to the fireplace. Gerald hadn't moved from his spot next to the fire, and as people began to gather around it Joshua sensed that he should have done the same.

The talk with Drew had been interesting though. They talked about The Way Side and how it had been built relatively recently. People had dwelled in The Valley for as long as anyone could remember, but it wasn't until a couple of hundred years ago that The Harbor was built, and The Way Side had been one of the first structures, along with a big barn that had been transformed into a greenhouse for growing vegetables and a dock for holding boats.

"No ship has ever arrived by ocean," Drew had said. "No one from the tundra either. The only way into The Valley is the river, and the only way out is the process by which a human body decays."

Joshua now laid curled up under a blanket some twenty feet from the fire. No one slept in the rooms here, they slept in piles. Big masses of people huddled together for warmth. An endless chorus of burping, farting, coughing, and insane mutterings; and for someone like Joshua, who had conditioned himself to sleep alone and wake at the slightest indication of another person's presence, he was in Hell. It must have been hours, but it felt like years. A stretching eternity of wobbling upon the edge of sleep. The kind of frustration that exhausts you more than hiking mountains all day.

In the end, he finally got up and found a bone-chilling room in which he could finally doze off. No heat, but there was also a good deal of quiet, and it wasn't like he wasn't used to sleeping in the cold anyway.

There were a few people in the room he was in but they were relatively quiet. There were some noises that rose up in the way of quiet grunts or rustling clothes but not enough to keep him awake indefinitely. The cold had crept into every inch of him but as long as he felt relatively safe he could make do.

The sleep was light and not entirely replenishing, but when he woke up the next morning to the sounds of people moving around and a thin filter of daylight brushing the dirty floor, he felt adequately rested. Joshua picked up the blanket he had found in the night, shook it out, rolled it up, and slung it over his shoulder.

"Got something for ya," Drew said as Joshua stepped through the doorway into the commons. People were shuffling about faster than they had the night before and while they didn't look particularly cheerful, they were at least excited. "Trader named Columbo died in the night, froze to death or something, who knows—anyway, he always slept on this big bag. We thought it was sand or acorns or something, he was kind of an off guy so we didn't give it much thought. But Krissy was making her rounds—seeing if anyone died in the night or anything—and first thing she does after flippn' his frozen body off the bag is cut it open. Guess what she finds?"

The smell had already struck Joshua and it was intoxicating, like a wind from a different world. He nodded at a clay cup on the counter with steam rising out of it.

"You betcha. Got us some nice, dark, aromatic coffee." Drew smiled wide and happy, but the scarred half of his face was so striking that the old wound betrayed every act of warmth or kindness with the underlying truth, making everything good he said sound like a bad lie. "Lucky it was Krissy that found it. Anyone else would have just up and taken it. This place is her life though. She's in back right now grinding the beans with a big rock."

"And she's just giving the stuff away?"

"For now she is, get the word out. People will come from all around, but when they get here tomorrow or days after, they gonna have to trade for it. They'll have been thinking about it so long that it won't matter. They'll give anything."

"You don't think people will be pissed," Joshua said skeptically.

"Oh they'll be pissed," and when Drew laughed a small dose of mischief crept into his eye. "But we hired some muscle." He tilted his head over to two hulking men crammed comedically into a wooden booth that was three sizes too small for them.

"How fast you think word'll spread?"

Drew smiled again, and this time it wasn't mischief in his eyes, but something else. Something Joshua found puzzling. "You ever been out there when the sun goes down? When it plunges behind the mountains faster than you ever thought it could and you're left standing in pitch darkness with no shelter? No sight?"

Joshua had, but he didn't answer.

"About that fast."

Joshua kept the warm, clay mug cupped snuggly in both of his hands as he stepped out into the frigid morning air. The temperature was low and a few small flakes fell light and lonesome to the ground. As he made his way down the path, he could already feel the increased activity around him. The buzz in the air.

Amazing.

He found it incredible how much a cup of hot coffee meant to these people. He also wasn't sure if he wanted to be here any longer. More people meant a higher chance of something terrible happening. Not to mention what it might mean to those monsters that had stalked him through the forest. Would they understand what it meant that people were going to flock to a single area? Were they hunting him or just hunting in general? Did it matter? Did anything?

Joshua thought about the fact that he thought he had almost died. *Did* die as far as he was concerned. No one could have survived what he had. Or should have.

It took a few minutes for him to find the person he was looking for, but eventually, he came across a ragged old man hunched over a small boat with a sail on it, his beard hanging down and touching the wooden gunnel.

"Gerald."

The man stopped what he was doing, turned and looked up into Joshua's face.

"What do ya have going on there?"

Gerald looked like he was thinking, but Joshua remembered the look on his face the previous night as he stared blankly into the fire, and he wasn't entirely sure that this wasn't the same look.

"She sits just a hair too high in the water. Gotta weigh her down if I don't want to tip over."

A thought struck Joshua. "Would another body help?"

Gerald had turned back to the boat, but upon hearing this he turned around again.

"I mean if I were to come with you? Would that help?"

The man breathed out and a small smile flicked across his face. "I suppose it would." He turned back and looked at the boat. "Problem is, I've already got a whole 'nother person's worth of weight," he pointed at some big stones that had been loaded onto the boat's wooden floor, "and she still sits too low."

"I see," Joshua waited a beat, a tad embarrassed. "So I suppose you already got someone else lined up to join you."

Gerald gave a short cough that could have been a laugh. "Actual-ly," he waited another awkward moment, making this feel like the most punctuated conversation Joshua had ever been involved in. "Actually, I had planned on asking you." He gave a nervous smile.

"Me?" Joshua raised his eyebrows. "You barely know me."

"Yeah, well." Gerald shrugged and looked like he was going to say more, but he didn't.

Now Joshua didn't feel as sure. The thought of getting away from The Harbor before more people showed up had seemed appealing at the time, but maybe he had been a bit too anxious. He didn't even know this old man, this strangely friendly vagabond that seemed to want nothing more than to cross the ocean and leave. And appar-ently, with Joshua.

"Tell ya what." Joshua gave Gerald a searching look. "I'm going to bum around here for a bit. Maybe grab some more coffee while I can. And I'll have a think on it." He nodded out towards the rough water. "That's some scary shit out there. And tell the truth, we have no idea how long we'd have to go before we reached anywhere, especially in that tiny thing." And Joshua meant it. The boat was hardly seaworthy. It may have been *pond*-worthy—perhaps even river-worthy—but the huge waves and ripping storms that raged over those waters looked like they could mulch a small twenty-foot boat into sawdust in less than a second.

"It's not that far," Gerald said hoarsely. Almost desperately.

"What's not that far?"

"I've seen a light. A flashing light. It flickers." He raised his right hand and quickly opened and closed it two times, mimicking flashes. "Two times. Always two times. It's out there, I've seen it when I've been out there. Always there. Always two times." He flashed his hand again. Looked nervously at the boat and back at Joshua.

"That's...interesting." Joshua's mind was turning. "Out there you say? How far about?"

Gerald shifted his weight, kneeling. "Couple hours maybe. Just with me rowing. We'd go faster with two."

"No sail?"

Gerald shrugged. "Maybe. Depends on the weather. It got chewed up by hail last time I was out there. Me too actually. Big chunks of ice, like-" He must have realized he wasn't exactly selling the idea with the promise of razor-sharp ice falling from the sky. "Well, I mean. I was okay. Sail got a bit beat up though." He looked up at Joshua sheepishly and a feeling of nostalgia passed through him.

"Yeah, well." Joshua turned and looked at the big building where more and more people were entering and exiting. "I'll think on it. Like I said." He turned away, then turned back again. "You want some coffee?"

Gerald looked at him incredulously. "Some *what*?"

"Coffee. Some guy died last night. Slept on a bag? Apparently, it was coffee. So now they're handing it out. Today only I guess. Gotta trade for it tomorrow."

"Columbo died?" Gerald looked genuinely upset. "How?"

"Dunno. Froze I suppose."

Gerald looked skeptical. "Froze? Columbo?"

"Yeah," Joshua said, now unsure.

"Huh," the old man looked down at his hand, balled it into a fist and then opened it again, stretching out the muscles. "Seemed okay yesterday."

"Well, that's what they said. So ya want some coffee?"

"Nah." Gerald shook his head slowly. "I'm ok, see if you can get some more fish though. I've got a lot stocked up but you can never have too much food out there." He stood up. "That is, if you plan on coming with of course." And again there was a pleading look in his eye, and again an uneasy sense of nostalgia and guilt passed through Joshua.

"Of course..." Joshua turned and started walking back up to The Way Side, then he stopped and looked back. "I'll let ya know either way though."

Gerald was looking back down at the boat, and he nodded without looking up.

What a strange man, Joshua thought. There was something about him that Joshua couldn't quite place. Something that made him feel genuinely uncomfortable.

Then there was the thing about the lights...

Joshua thought back to a cold night a long time ago. A night when he prayed that no one was out on a midnight cruise along the ocean shore. He had turned off all of the boathouse lights, but occasionally one would flash two times like a flash-bulb from a camera. It had shocked him out of his reverie the first time. Thought that it actually *had* been a camera—someone who had snuck up on him. Caught him sitting there on the dock, a blood-stained silhouette.

He remembered standing there and looking out at the ocean. He also thought he saw something white out there like a sail, or maybe a whale surfacing briefly before it plunged back down into the depths. He had never seen a whale from the cabin dock, but he thought that he would have liked to—thought that, maybe if he could see one of those majestic creatures out in the wild, that everything would be made right again.

But he didn't. The night had been jet-black after that, except of course for the light. The light that, for the briefest of moments, illuminated a man about to take the first step into a new life.

Joshua found Drew handing out cups of coffee in the commons of The Way Side. A long line of smelly travelers clothed in hanging rags and dirty furs stood sniffling and fidgeting before the bar, while the scarred man behind the counter poured and distributed the clay mugs.

A fair amount of the people in line gave Joshua dirty and nervous looks as he passed them up on his way to the counter. "Drew, you gotta sec?" Joshua didn't expect him to be able to leave at this moment and was surprised when he turned to address the woman back in the kitchen.

"Krissy, can you take over for me?"

The short, feral looking woman that Joshua had seen the day before came waddling out, flexing her fingers.

"Just for a few minutes," Drew said.

She gave a curt nod and walked over to where Drew had been standing and began to pour more cups from a huge clay jug with a crude, wooden spigot inserted into a hole in the bottom. Three more jugs stood lined up on the countertop.

"Let's head over here," Drew grabbed his mug, waited for Krissy to fill another, and then handed that one to Joshua. They walked over to one of the tight wooden booths dug into the wall and Drew kicked the boot of a man sleeping on the bench. "Gordon. Hey." The man slowly woke and peered out of a single open eye. "There's an open spot by the fire just now."

Suddenly alive, the man got up quickly and hurried over to the fire. There weren't actually any open spots, but he pushed and snuggled in, making one for himself anyway. Drew and Joshua sat down on the wooden seats.

"So, ya got me for a sec. What's going on?"

Joshua thought a moment before answering him. "I uh—this is going to sound a little weird but," he waved his hand around vaguely, "what is this place?"

Drew had a look of uncertainty on his face. "You mean The Way Side?"

"No," Joshua said quickly. "Uh—I mean," he pursed his lips, "I mean, this place is strange, right? The Valley?"

Comprehension dawned on Drew. " Ah yes, The Valley. It is a little different isn't it?"

"I mean, I thought that I...ya know..."

Drew sat and waited.

"Died. I guess." Joshua felt a little stupid. "I tried to leave The Valley, but my canoe—anyway, I fell in the water, and next thing I know, I'm being hauled back out some thirty miles downstream."

Drew simply nodded, waited for a moment, and then asked: "Is there a question in there?"

"Yeah," Joshua said. He inhaled. "Drew, what do you think Hell is?"

A smile flashed over Drew's face, like a silent chuckle. "Hell?" He blew out a breath and leaned back, thinking. "I'm not quite sure I'd say this is Hell. Look at that guy over there." He pointed at an ancient-looking man receiving a cup of coffee. "Look at the look on that man's face. I can't imagine that sort of thing is allowed in Hell. No, I'll tell you what I think Hell is."

Joshua leaned back and listened.

"A few decades ago—sixty years maybe, before my time—we had a long string of amiable weather. No storms, no snow, the wind was steady but not brutal like it has been lately. Anyway, these four guys, three Northerners and a Southerner, they decide that the water is calm enough, so they're going to try and sail out into that ocean. See what's on the other side, yeah?"

Joshua nodded.

"Well, they sail out. The weather keeps, everything seems fine, the water is uncharacteristically smooth. Problem is, the wind dies. Dead calm. So they just float."

"Let me guess, they run out of food and water?"

Drew pointed a finger at Joshua's chest and made a shooting noise with his mouth. "You got it. So they're out there for days. Run out of food, run out of water, run out of patience for each other. Now, let me ask you, you ever drank salt water before?"

Joshua shook his head.

"It's classic irony. You're stranded out there surrounded by water, and you think you're about to die of dehydration. Makes no sense. Except it does. Because salt water is practically a different substance. The salt makes it undrinkable, you can't see it if you just look at the water, but its there, and it makes a difference."

Joshua nodded, but he wasn't exactly following. "And what does this have to do with Hell?"

Drew spread his arms. "We are an ocean, and Hell is the salt. There's a little bit in all of us. You can compare us to what people think God looks like: tall man, big beard, all that. They say we're made in his image, that we look just like him. In fact, you might not even be able to tell the difference if a man like you or me were to stand right next to him."

"But there is a difference," Joshua said. "That's what you're saying right? The unseen salt. The Hell—it's inside of us?"

"Correct." Drew looked pleased with himself. "The difference between water and salt water."

Joshua thought for a second. "So what happened to those four men, the ones who drank the—Hell—or the *proverbial* Hell, I guess?"

Drew smiled a comfortable smile. "They went mad. They became sick, hungry, wrathful, and eventually," he spread his hands apart, "dead."

The pair of them sat there quietly before Drew broke the silence again. "You're wondering what'll happen if you go out there. On the ocean. Gerald wants to take you right?"

"He does," Joshua said, half thinking to himself.

"My advice? Don't. I'd be wary of Gerald. He's...*different* than most of the others around here." Drew interlocked his fingers and pushed his hand out, cracking his knuckles. "Then again, maybe you'll just end up back here, right? If you die?" He laughed. Joshua didn't.

Joshua tilted his head in question. "How do you know about those four guys? If they all died, I mean. Who was left to tell the story?"

"Well, *you* died right?"

A shiver ran up Joshua's spine.

15

OVIN

This was it. As soon as he had laid eyes on the scene of carnage, Ovin had known that this was why they did what they did. It's not that serving in the army or a police force was less lucrative—it's that it was less effective. They'd be hamstrung by policies and weighed down by bureaucracies and huge chains of command. Right now, Ovin and his hunters could make a snap decision to pursue The Pack until the ends of the earth. They would find them, and when they tore them to pieces they wouldn't have to stage any sort of firefight or submit any reports. They'd just burn the fucking place down and walk away. The tape would be sent off, and before long they'd be doing the same thing to Espina himself. What those guys had done to those villagers, sewing them to animals like that?

Ovin would personally watch that man shit himself and die.

He knew the others felt it too. Raquel was still cool, still calm, but she was moving faster. Pushing herself harder. Ovin could see the focus and determination in her gait.

On the other end of the spectrum there as Russ, he wouldn't shut up about what he was going to do to those *"bandejos,"* which was apparently the only Spanish word he knew other than "casa." For someone who had grown up so close to Mexico, he knew surprisingly little of the language. Ever since they had gotten up that morning to hike the last fifteen miles to the small town that lay just outside the entrance to the valley, Russ did nothing but mutter obscenities to himself as he trudged along. In fact, Ovin was a little unsure about how he'd react to the next people they found. Russ wasn't in a particularly friendly mood, and if they hoped to get any information out of the town's people about the valley, they'd have to be polite and grease the wheels with a bit of free food and supplies. That or resort to torture.

Ovin knew the pitfalls of torture though, especially on a job like this. He had seen it before. It may seem like a good and justifiable idea at the time, but a while later the idea of the ends justifying the means begins to warp people's perception of what exactly that "end" was supposed to look like. If your goal is to stop someone that does terrible things, and you do terrible things to accomplish it, you've immediately filled the vacuum left by the perpetrators' absence. Suddenly those mutilated bodies that turned your stomach so much in the beginning look a lot like the ones you've left in your wake.

Ovin had seen all of the outcomes of people who tortured for a living. Some gave their lives to drugs and alcohol; some to God, charity, or repentance; and some gave themselves to their own weapons— that last bullet fired just for them. The worst, Ovin thought, was the most common. They simply stopped caring. It was like seeing someone's dynamic personality, filled with all of the wonderful and contradicting landscapes of hope and despair and love and hate and selfishness and servitude just get bulldozed—just absolutely obliterated and flattened into a frozen wasteland where only selfishness and cynicism thrive.

Torture was the one thing Ovin always sought to avoid. Not for the sake of the intended targets, but for the wellbeing of everyone under his command. This thing with the dogs—it felt just. But after this—after Espina—he wouldn't be doing it again. He was already seeing the effect it was having on his soldiers. He'd have to tread lightly now.

The dogs had been working the path ahead since dawn. Wesley protested to the speed at which they were traveling because he didn't feel he could adequately scout the land ahead, but he kept pace regardless. They were moving at a pretty good clip and Ovin didn't want them to lose their momentum. The Pack obviously knew they were coming so the only thing they had on their side now was their drive and the fact that, once they found them, they could choose when to attack. If they waited and took their time, there was a chance that they'd enter the valley too late and never find them. They'd lose their line, their advantage; people who had seen them would begin to forget and information would begin to dry up. They needed to hit them hard and they needed to hit them now.

Russ was flushed red beside Ovin. He had moved up, his rifle unslung the whole time, and now he was keeping stride with him and Raquel, which broke the formation they had agreed upon. He was fire support, and should, therefore, be further back, ready to spread out and lay down covering fire.

"Slow down there bud, we still got a ways to go." Ovin's voice was low and gentle. He had already given Russ a tongue lashing, and he far from regretted it, but now was the time to reel him back in, show support. Russ had to follow orders and he would, but right now another verbal beatdown would do nothing but harm their relationship. He wanted Russ's respect and his trust; not his hatred, not his sympathy, not his friendship. What Ovin needed Russ to do was follow him with everything in his heart, not because he was afraid not to, but because he wanted to. Granted, there would be times when they would disagree on strategy, but when push came to shove, Ovin would always win those battles.

Russ remained silent, but he looked less sure than he had a second ago. Ovin guessed that he was trying to figure out if he wanted him to simply take it easier or to fall back in line. And as soon as he made the right decision and started to fall back, Ovin stopped him.

"Actually, why don't you hang up here for just a minute. Raquel, can you take support for a moment?"

Raquel gave a quick nod and immediately moved back. No hassle, no objection, Ovin truly didn't deserve a soldier as good as her.

Russ and Ovin walked in silence for a moment, their boots making light scuffs on the ground. The sun overhead turned everything into a harsh washboard of browns and greys. Ovin broke the silence.

"What's your plan when we get to town?"

Russ looked over at him and didn't answer.

Ovin let him squirm for a second and then continued. "Someone there must have seen The Pack come through. Any ideas on how to get information out of them." He could feel Russ's anger beside him. Not towards *him*, but towards their query. He knew that Russ instantly wanted to beat it out of whoever he found, but that he sensed the trap laid by Ovin's words and considered his own before speaking.

"Maybe ask first. Straight up."

"Could work. There are certain people who respond to that sort of thing. I don't think these will be that kind of people though. Remember those guys we came across back in that town when we were looking for Trixie? These are going to be those kinds of people. Maybe not as immediately violent, but they're going to be wary of us. Especially if one of Espina's kill squads has just been through."

"Cowards if you ask me. They'll open fire on us, but not the people who are cutting their daughters' throats and hanging their sons from bridges with steel wire? Makes no fucking sense."

"I know what you mean, but to them, we're still outsiders. We're still people they don't know stepping into their homes with loaded guns. No matter what we try and do, we will always be an invading force to them. Espina's guys they know. They at least find them predictable, think that it's a domestic problem, something they can deal with. They're wrong, but that's how they think."

Russ nodded but didn't look convinced.

"Another thing is, it's not like these people *haven't* tried to fight them. There are all sorts of factions spread out over this place with no other objective than killing them. But they need funding. They need supplies. Soon enough, they're not only Espina's enemies, they're his competition, and before long they're doing the same crazy shit he is."

"That's not what I mean though," Russ said. "I mean, why don't they all just rise up and throw his ass out?"

"Well, first of all, organizing that would be tough. You ever try to pick a leader for something? Unless one presented themselves, they'd never be able to coordinate anything. That's why we've got all of these factions out here. A bunch of people want the same thing, but they can't agree on the specifics. In addition, Espina's got spies and informants everywhere. People are afraid to talk, afraid to take action. Sure, they could theoretically organize to throw Espina out, but who has time to think about that when you've got mouths to feed and kids to clothe? Espina's not an *immediate* threat you see? At least, not like he would be if you started getting rowdy and trying to plan an overthrow. So what everyone does is they just keep their heads down, because chances are, if you finally work up the courage to start some shit, the guy next door won't be at that point yet. He'll still be worried about his wife and kids. Then all of a sudden you find your whole family blindfolded in the town square with machine guns being loaded behind your backs. See?"

"Yeah, I guess." Russ had assumed a face of disgust and impatience. "It just seems like a big contradiction to me. No one will fight because they'll get killed, and they get killed because no one will fight."

"I know, it seems stupid, but you can't think of people like that. I know what you mean though. The people who just want to live here all want the same thing, so why don't they make it happen? But the thing is, they can all think the same thing, but they can't immediately know if everyone else is thinking the same thing. And it's that period of time where you're trying to get everyone on the same page that people like The Pack swoop in and make an example of you."

Ovin paused for a moment, and they walked silently with their thoughts.

"Let me put it this way: you ever stand in line for something? Like, you're all waiting to move and then when you finally can it seems like it takes forever for the person in front of you to go?"

Russ nodded.

"It's like that. Theoretically, everyone could all move forward as soon as the path in front was clear. Everyone moves at once. But can you imagine the kind of trust that would take? If just one person hesitates, everyone behind them will come crashing into the person in front of them. So what do they do? They wait for the person in front of them to take a step and put a reasonable amount of space between them before they start walking. So instead of everyone moving forward at once, the second person has to wait for the first person to start and the third person for the second. The movement ripples backward as cause and effect, rather than everyone just doing what they should."

Ovin could feel his throat getting dry from talking so much, but he continued. "I think that's why we have people like Espina. No one knows what anyone else is thinking. There's no sympathy, no empathy, no understanding. There's just people trying to do what's right for them and trying to ignore the damage in their wake. It's people killing people because those people killed people. It's cyclical and outrageous, but there's no way around it. People going to do fucked up shit, then others gonna try and fix it by doing the same. It's a dog eat dog world out there, and with this many dogs, everyone gets eaten."

Russ was quiet for a really long time, and just when Ovin thought he wasn't going to reply, he said quietly, "Trent tell you why I'm out here, sir?"

The "sir" caught Ovin off guard. It wasn't something he demanded from the men and women that followed him, so it felt extra meaningful when he did hear it.

"Can't say he did."

"Dad didn't just want to make a man out of me, he's trying to give me some sort of closure."

Everything immediately snapped together in Ovin's mind. No one ever really knew why Cruz contracted out to have people hunt down Espina and his men, but there had been rumors about something real bad that had gone down a while back, and when Ovin heard the tone of Russ's voice, he knew that he had lost someone, which meant that Cruz had too.

"It was my mom. Didn't even do nothing. Was just in the wrong place at the wrong time. She took a stray bullet when she was down here with a mission group. That's the sort of person she was." Russ's voice cracked. "I was going to have a brother. Dad said—he said that she should stay home—that it wasn't just herself she had to worry about."

Ovin nodded, still moving forward.

"But she wanted what you were talking about. She thought every-thing would be better if you just helped out—if people saw you helping and could think to themselves 'wow, maybe there is some hope.' She said she didn't want to be that mom who only worries about her own kids—her own life—while the world burned around them. She said that that was how things got bad."

Ovin nodded. Russ didn't need to finish: *and look where it got her. Where it got us.*

"So your dad wanted you to come here and—what? Learn that she was wrong?"

"Yeah, something like that," Russ said. "I think it may have been a little more...good natured. I think he wanted me to—I don't know, find some closure I guess. Like I said. I don't know, maybe he just wanted me to see the world that he saw. Give me *perspective.*"

"That's a peculiar dad you have there. Mine would've done the opposite," Ovin said, steering the conversation. He waited a beat before talking, trying to decide if he was about to make the right move or not. "My dad wanted me to be as far from any sort of blood-shed as possible. I don't think it was because he thought it would mess me up, but because he felt guilty."

"Why would he feel guilty?" Russ asked.

Ovin exhaled. "When I was a kid, we were on our way back to our cabin. Sunny afternoon, birds chirping, all that. But there were these guys following us. I was like...6, so I had no idea what was going on, but my dad knew. We kept getting further and further out there into the boonies, and they just kept following. Well, long story short, those guys were going to rob us. That's what he says at least. But before they could-" Ovin looked around, changing direction slightly. "I was in the back of the car in the driveway, watching over the back of the car seat, and I see him talking to them through their open car window, and suddenly he just—well, he pulled this hunting knife out of his belt and jammed it through the opening."

Russ had a look of amazement on his face.

"Guy inside bled all over the seat. Another guy jumped out and ran around to—I don't know, do *something*—and well, my dad killed him too. Just stabbed him right up through the gut before anyone could do or say anything. Pulled the knife out and stabbed him again. Did it probably—three more times? Shit, it was all over. They were dead."

Ovin breathed out through his nose. "It all fell apart after that. Just—fucking everything. I remember sitting in that awful smelling station wagon that those guys had driven in. We drove out to some swamp where my dad used to duck hunt and pushed the car in. At first it didn't look like it was going to sink, we thought maybe it wasn't deep enough, but eventually, the muck crept further and further up the windows until the whole thing was submerged. Bodies were piled one on top of the other in the backseat."

"Your dad brought you with?" Russ asked.

"Yeah. I asked him about that before I left home. Apparently, he did it automatically, said he was afraid for me and needed to keep me in his sight the whole time. He had never really been like that, always gave me a decent amount of space as a kid, but after that, he became overbearingly attentive."

"We kept it from my mom for a little while, though she could tell something was different. She pried it out of him one night and probably wished she hadn't. I couldn't have seen it ending any other way though." Ovin paused for a second, thinking. "I have little fragments of memory from the time before that day—little pictures of my parents doting over each other—*loving* each other. A secret like that though...ya know it wasn't the secret that did it—I'm convinced that my mom would have helped my dad bare something like that no matter what—it was the way my dad withdrew from her. He became a stone that she could squeeze nothing from, a mass of worry and paranoia."

"Did she leave him?" Russ had something in his voice, and Ovin briefly wondered if divorce was something you could even comprehend after one of your parents had died like Russ's had.

"That's hard to say. An armchair psychologist would say that he left her long before, but I don't know. It broke her though. The whole situation. To love someone that refuses to acknowledge you for so many years. It makes you wonder what love can endure, because her love was the purest I'd ever seen and it still failed. Makes you wonder if it was ever love at all, if there even is such a thing."

Russ nodded. Ovin guessed that he had some opinions on the situation but he withheld them.

"I left maybe two weeks after she did. It feels like a contradiction, like some fucked up joke, that it wasn't until he became terrified of losing us that he actually did." What Ovin was about to say next, he had thought many times but had only ever said out loud once, and it was to Raquel after drinking too much one night. They were curled up under a blanket like always, his face buried in her hair.

"I think I hate him."

The look on Russ's face indicated that he wasn't sure if he had heard him right or not. "Hate him?"

"Yeah. Just—what's done was done, ya know? Two guys strolled up when they shouldn't have, we don't even know if they *were* going to rob us, my dad just said he *felt* it. Whatever that means. It's just all so fucking stupid, but it's hard to explain. I just—all I want is for us to go back to that little snapshot I have in my head, of the perfect family."

"I mean he *killed* some guys though. *People.* I can't imagine anything would be the same after that," Russ said.

"What I mean is, he should have just let it the fuck *go*. Instead, he dwelled on it. Let it consume him. It became like this place he would go and live in instead of at home. He was around us, but he wasn't *with* us. He was off in his own self-made Hell somewhere, worrying about what he had done, or what was going to happen."

Unsure what to say next, the two of them plodded on towards the town that had begun to loom up before them. A few moments passed, and when Ovin turned to look at Russ they knew each other. Two kids from homes broken by unforeseen violence, they set out to commit violence of their own, not in spite of that violence, but because of it.

People could now be seen moving in the buildings ahead. Some hanging clothes in the windows, others traveling hurriedly through the streets in search of everyday supplies. But all of them had their eyes on the approaching group, seeing them not for what they looked like, which was a squad of soldiers, but for what they were, which was a pack of hunters. Killers.

Everyone was on their guard.

No one made any immediate moves towards the strangers as they strode in, mainly because it was observed and telegraphed that the majority of them did not enter the town, only two men and a woman. The others—The pack of dogs included—remained on the outskirts, settling into an outcrop of brush and rock, huddling the dogs together and resting for a few hours.

Ovin and Raquel entered the weary town as they had planned, the only alteration being that they brought Russ along. They had connected back on the trail, but right now Ovin still didn't trust him not to explode on someone who stumbled into their camp. He was still an unknown variable, as he had always been, and Ovin felt better with him by his side where he could keep a proverbial leash on him.

The first thing they did was to go buy some vegetables from a few of the street vendors. They needed to set a friendly, noninvasive tone. And they legitimately needed the food. The vendors traded their wares with solemnity and efficiency, and when they had traded for the third time Ovin asked where they could get a drink. After speaking with them in hushed Spanish for a few brief seconds, the three of them left and made their way to a single-story building near the center of town with a roof that wasn't completely dilapidated and only had steel bars on the windows as opposed to boards.

The three of them were met with nervous glances when they entered. A few people left immediately while others watched with looks of caution.

When Ovin asked for a drink, the bartender poured brown liquor into a glass and spat out a number that was most likely double what regulars paid. Ovin reached into his coat pocket and pulled out some paper bills. They hadn't brought their rifles into town, but when Ovin put his hand in his coat the bartender watched closely and was rewarded with the dull flash of the Glock in its shoulder holster. It was nonchalant, hardly threatening, but the way it was done settled all doubt: mercenary. Not rigid enough for a DEA agent, too practiced for a tourist.

Mercs were unknown variables in these parts. They could have been hired out by almost anyone—anyone, that is, that could afford mercenary work, which narrowed it down to cartels and people trying to stop cartels. People were afraid of speaking though.

In Spanish, Ovin asked if they had seen any enforcers come through—anyone associated with Espina's gang. At the use of the name, the bartender hesitated, but it could have been for a number of reasons. Perhaps he was trying to decide if he should lie or not. Maybe he was wondering if he was being tested. Maybe, this was some sort of veiled threat and he had yet to interpret it as such. Or maybe, he was just scared of the very name.

Predictably, he shook his head. It was a long shot, but any information that Ovin could use to pinpoint exactly where they were heading would be helpful. However—he glanced around the room—

he hadn't actually expected this many people to still be in town, especially with a kill squad operation just miles away.

The information they had received from other people was vague. There was simply a group of four people on the move: two men and two women. Small for a kill squad, but apparently they were efficient. They had been strangers in those places, but here they'd be known. And Ovin wanted to find out where they were going.

Raquel had her back to the bar and was casually probing with her eyes as Russ strode slowly around, not making eye contact with anyone.

As Raquel slowly observed the people around them, Ovin got a strange feeling, a sort of sixth sense warning bell. Something about the bar, the town, the dead bodies, all of it lined up in a certain way and there wasn't any sort of discernible pattern that felt out of the ordinary, but in that second he gave pause.

What was it?

He looked at Raquel. Her face was as impassive as ever. It was observant, vigilant, and tenderly questioning all at once. *What's up?* The small downturn of the mouth, slight furrowing of the brow. Her face looked like some sort of teetering vase, about to fall.

"Hey." The voice was high and garbled, like that of some sort of bird. "You looking for El Paquette?"

All three of them turned, and with that, the bartender did what he was paid to do. He reached underneath the towel below the bar, drew out a small sawn-off pump shotgun, pointed it at Raquel's face, and blew it into a thousand shattered pieces.

The bar erupted into chaos.

Even as Raquel was falling, a solitary arm attached to a stunned body was reaching absentmindedly into a coat; pulling out a Glock; aiming it at the frightened bartender's face who was too stunned by his own actions to acknowledge the matte-black pistol before it;

leveling it and making a tiny, black hole below his right eye. A single dark and smoking teardrop.

The sound of the shot from the Glock was tiny in Ovin's ear, a distant tick of something falling far, far away. His mind was numb and his eyes uncomprehending, even as his body did the work. It pulled the trigger two more times before the man behind the bar hit the ground. Then Ovin was vaulting up over the bar and crouching down behind it. He popped up immediately and swept the room. Everyone was either running out the door, crawling under a table, or in Russ's case turning around frantically in every direction before settling on pistol-whipping the man who had called to them in order to draw their attention.

After less than a minute, almost all of the bar's patrons had scrambled out except for Ovin, Russ, and the man Russ was now holding at gunpoint.

"Where are they?" Russ was screaming. He had a black Beretta 9mm pressed against the man's glistening temple. The man trembled and seemed unable to speak, tears rolling down his face.

Slowly and carefully, Ovin walked out from behind the bar. He looked down at Raquel. Her face was fragmented in a sea of blood and tissue, her once elegant nose that swooped down like a dove to rest on the perch of her lips was now hanging by a flap of skin and cartilage from the top of the bridge. Teeth lay white and shimmering across the floor like the delicate flakes of ash or a first snow. Ovin could feel his grief huge and heavy inside him, but his training kept it contained. It could wait 'til later.

He took five big strides over to Russ and the man he was attempting to question. Kneeling down next to him, Ovin spoke calmly and quietly. "Were you paid to divert our attention? Hey-" The man's cheek had a gash on the side and his head pointed down at the floor; Ovin reached up with a finger and tilted his chin towards him. At first, the man flinched away, but when he wasn't hit he turned slowly back and eventually made eye contact with Ovin. Ovin asked again, slower this time: "Were you paid to divert our attention?"

The man had already demonstrated an ability to speak english, but Ovin wasn't sure if he wouldn't have trouble with the word "divert." He looked up at Russ after not receiving an answer and Russ lifted the pistol for another blow across the man's already bleeding cheek.

"Wait, wait, wait!" The man said the words so fast they almost sounded like one. "They threatened me. They said they'd kill my brother and his family if I didn't help them." He spoke with a strong Latin-American accent. "All they say was, 'get your attention. Ask if you was looking for El Paquette.' So I did. They didn't say what would happen." Ovin watched him glance at Raquel's lifeless body. "They didn't say anyone would die."

"You probably guessed though, right? I mean you had to have." Ovin's voice was cold.

The man waited a second before answering, then simply shrugged and shook his head, as if he truly didn't know what to say.

"Where are they?" Ovin asked.

The man squeezed his eyes shut. "The motel I think. That's where they usually stay." He opened his eyes and then looked at the door, as if he was expecting them to come in at any moment. His words summoning them like a pack of demons.

"What room?" Russ asked the question.

"I don't know the number," the man said nervously, his jowls shaking as he spoke. Russ pressed the muzzle of the pistol into his ear. "The back corner. There's an alley that run's behind it that they can use as an escape route. They have security in front to protect them. Probably a few in the room with them."

Ovin looked at him with hard eyes. "Why does a kill squad need security?"

The man's eyes darted up at Russ and back down at Ovin. It was clear that he wouldn't tell them, but not Ovin thought, because he didn't know. They had reached a point where the man's mental state was closing down, giving way to the fear and forfeiting all knowledge and rational thought. He was breathing faster and faster, trying to make words but failing. It didn't matter. What mattered now was that they knew what they were up against and that they had to move.

Ovin took a slow and steady breath before speaking next. "Ok. Thank you." He stood up and glanced at Russ. "Go home to your brother. Have nothing more to do with Espina or his men."

The man's eyes filled with relief. He shifted his weight to his shaking knee to stand up.

Ovin looked away as Russ shot him in the back of the head.

16

THE PACK

A storm raged up the coast. Not a storm of wind and water and ice, but of claws and teeth. Of fire and wrath. All things composed of flesh knelt before it in a hissing puddle of sizzling blood and burning hair. They had received the message and were on their way. There was no telling how long the man would be there. By this point, The Pack's anger and vengeance had spun up into an unquenchable storm, and when they burst out into a clearing that lay right outside of The Harbor and a few people witnessed their approach, they quaked with terror and stood rooted to the spot until they were slain.

The whole town died.

Some were able to flee as the black wolves stalked from building to building in search of their prey, but most of them were struck down and torn apart. Their torturous lives ended in a fear so palpable that it spread like a wind throughout The Valley on the lips of the survivors. And when men and women woke in the night with terror in their hearts of the things they thought they had dreamt, they carried it with them, night-to-night. Death-to-death. The cycles of violence in The Valley accelerating as all things do before their climax, their end, their rebirth.

One man stood outside of The Way Side as it burned to the ground. He thought he could smell an acrid tinge of burning coffee beans in the air, but it was likely his imagination. The stench of burnt flesh was so strong it made the strongest of hearts want to vomit. Made the weakest of hearts want to stop. And made the darkest of hearts want to feed.

He stood displeased outside of his burning home. The large wolf in front of him stood rigid and bristling, its mouth slack and billowing smoke through the saber-like teeth that hung unevenly like massive shards of broken glass.

"He's not here," breathed the monster, it's voice like the roar of an inferno.

"No. He's not," said Drew. "You're too late."

"Too late," it roared. "We traveled on the back of time itself, whose hands wield no power here. The only power here is pain and it is boiling over."

"He is gone." Drew kicked a chunk of ice. "They *both* are."

At this the black wraith threw its head back and swung its clawed hands to the ground, digging up massive clumps of dirt in its fury that boiled and turned to glass in the dry and frigid air around them, the heat from the burning buildings having somewhat lessened in the recent minutes as the fire burned down. The howl was a hurricane from the mouth of some exiled titan.

"What would you like me to tell them if they come back?" Drew's cheerful tone betrayed his annoyance.

The wolf lumbered over him, raised its paw, but then stopped. It tilted its head. "If they have escaped us then time is on their side. If time is on their side, then they will not return at all. No bodies will be plucked from the ocean to stride through more bitter days. No hands will burst through dirt and ice to seize the bounty of numb despair that exists perpetually and unrivaled in this land. If their grievances are settled—if they have embraced *death* with open arms, then they are truly gone." And then, the coal-black mouth pinched and distorted in a serrated smile. "But, if even one shall return, then we will hunt him and kill him unceasingly until he goes to The God's Eye. No one comes back from the ocean a better man. They either escape or become slaves. And if either of these two become slaves, they become *our* slaves. We will dwell in them like the molten heart within the careless earth. They will be hopeless. They will go to The God's Eye. And when they look out over the landscape, they will drown in it."

"Tell me," Drew said. "If you know so much about the-" he tilted his head in search of the right word, "-*rules*, for lack of a better term, then why don't *you* leave."

And at this, the wolf leaned in close to the man. "Because-" Drew didn't see so much as he felt the grin. "Because this is our *home* now. What that old man did to us opened our *eyes*. You might balk at the rules of this place—where time and death are unpredictable—but this is the only place where the rules actually make sense. The Valley is existence stripped to its core."

The answer had been expected. Of course, this was their home, just as it was Drew's, but a part of him felt a sliver of doubt. Something deep inside of him flickered with a desire to just let it all go. But then he remembered—remembered what that man had done to his family—his *only* family. How he had ripped it apart so needlessly. How he had sent his mother into a fit of despair that he could only observe from afar and was powerless to help. He remembered all of the old hatred that had dwelt with him for so long and submitted to it like a man submits to hunger, for both find their hosts in the hearts of normal people, no matter the amount of their wealth nor the ease of their lives. He submitted to the only open arms he had ever discerned in a cruel and bitter world, the arms of justice—of the promise that the wages of violence are always violence, and that as the perpetrators of suffering send pain into the world, so shall their pain be their only legacy as it walks from heart to heart. From soul to soul.

Drew—or the man that had called himself drew since he had arrived here—looked up into the burning eyes of the demon in front of him and thought that the fire there was so brilliant that it couldn't have existed without some equally as brilliant counterpart. Drew knew that the world existed in polarities, and wondered if there was not some other place where another part of this man existed.

Or another part of himself for that matter.

17

JOSHUA

They had set sail the following day. After discussing how to steer the sail and bail water and what they would need and how long it should take to get to where they were going, they checked and double-checked their supplies, climbed into the disconcertingly small boat, and then set off. The water hadn't been glassy smooth like it had been when the men in Drew's story had set off, but the water was manageable as long as two people steered.

The sail was fixed to the center of the boat, and they had gone through how to use it properly, but Gerald was still hesitant. One of the reasons he was nervous—aside from the possibility of the sail being literally ripped off of the boat by gale-force winds—was that it was also a huge signal. Granted, no one had ever seen anyone out here besides those that had departed from The Harbor, but a lifetime of never being too careful made both Gerald and Joshua hesitant to announce their presence to anyone within seeing distance—not so long as they could propel the boat with the oars. Sure, it was more work, but the last thing that they wanted to do was to have their fragile plan smashed apart by something easily prevented. There were enough unknown variables as it was going on this little adventure, and it would be ridiculous to be halted by a known one.

It seemed slow-going at first. Joshua had made a pretty decent recovery after being pulled from the water, but he didn't exactly use all of the muscles needed to row a boat on a daily basis. Five minutes in and his back was starting to burn. He turned around to look at the shore to see how far they had gone and was shocked to find it still startlingly close. He wasn't sure if this was another trick of The Valley, or if he was just weak as shit. Either way, he had no problem asking Gerald if they could slow their pace a little.

Time passed and Joshua slowly received a second wind. He could already feel where blisters were going to form on his hands, but it was a small price to pay for a possible escape from The Valley. The two men fell into a steady rhythm and Joshua was impressed with the way that a man that looked almost twice his age seemed to be handling the boat with ease. The motion put Joshua into a trance-like state, and after an unknowable amount of time, he came back to his senses and turned around.

It was all gone. The Harbor, The Valley, everything. There was nothing visible in any direction except for the rolling backs of waves that, as far as he knew, could have come from way out in an eternal ocean and been cruising forward for centuries, breaking for nothing and no one as it single-mindedly traveled like a steady edge of an ever-expanding circle. The ripple effect of a single stone being dropped into all the world's water, its energy fleeing in every direction like birds from fire.

For the first time since they had departed, Joshua felt the tiniest bit scared. Fear was something to be honed and tempered, an accelerant that added a healthy dose of caution to one's steps and stayed the hand at the right moments. People who were fearless were more often than not, the bright and burning stars that walk the earth for mere moments before being swallowed up by every single thing that they should have been afraid of, for all of existence is an unknowable maw with unfathomable power that can strike you from its face at any time without warning. The fear that Joshua now felt, however, was different. It had no outlet, no purpose—it was slowly becoming a wailing alarm that attempted to signify a danger that was both immediately observable and wholly unavoidable. It was the pain that follows the loss of one's own hand, as if you hadn't noticed and perhaps there was some way of remedying the situation. Joshua sunk down ever so slightly into the hollowed-out cup of the boat, as if he were some liquid about to be sloshed out.

"How long do you 'spose we've been rowing?" Joshua asked, trying to find the sun through the thick overcast and failing.

"I don't know really," Gerald said. "Tell the truth, I'm not sure it much matters out here."

"How do you mean?"

"Well, let's just say, I've spent a lot of time out here rowing around. And some of it should have been daylight and wasn't, and some of it should have been night, but, well..."

"You do a lot of traveling then," Joshua asked. He felt a certain kinship with Gerald, something he hadn't felt with many men. And he had begun to formulate a theory as to why that was.

And it terrified him.

If Joshua was correct as to who was currently sitting in front of him, then perhaps he was about to find his way out of The Valley after all. Just not in the way he had intended. He felt like a naked pupil set within the dark grey iris of the ocean around him—an eye, that as the saying went, was about to be removed for another.

"I do," Gerald said, and as he adjusted in his seat Joshua felt the same twinge of memory prod him. He was becoming more and more certain, that the man sitting in front of him was the reason he was here, the reason that he had drowned but been spat out of the ocean kicking and sputtering just the same.

"I think we all do our fair of traveling in the world Gerald. Whether it be literally moving from place to place, or from person to person, or even idea to idea." Joshua leaned forward. "Tell me, do you think you've found what you've been looking for?"

Gerald turned slowly in his seat and looked back at Joshua's grim face. His eyes were tired but seemed nervous, uncertain.

"I think—I am not certain, but I think I am close," said the man in front of Joshua, the man he had known for no more than mere seconds but had been with him his entire life.

"I like to think we both are," said the man Joshua had murdered.

Silence accompanied them like a third person as they rowed. The sky remained as opaque and impassive as ever as the sea bounced the small boat up and down. Joshua thought that he had begun to hear the cracks and moans of the boards that held the boat together and realized that that wasn't a sound that had accompanied them prior. He looked out at the water and noticed that they were bouncing a little higher than usual and falling just a bit farther down, the surf spraying outward and misting both of their faces. Joshua tried to remember the shade of grey that had set the tone for their journey earlier that day, and though he couldn't be certain, he would have said that it had been a bit lighter than it was now.

He was also getting colder. The water had been splashing up and spraying him almost constantly and now there was a noticeable wind scything layers of heat off of his body with every passing second. The ocean was relatively new to him except for what he remembered from his cabin days, but even then he seldom ventured out on it. He would stay huddled in his little cove and weather the storms in comfortable the surroundings. It wasn't until he found himself pitted against the occupants of The Valley that he had begun to learn about weather patterns—what the wind could tell you and what certain clouds looked like. And though it was hard for him to truly grasp any sort of distance out here, he was now certain that he could see some black thunderheads roiling out of the West.

If his experience in The Valley had taught him anything about clouds that looked like that, it was that he should find shelter and find it soon. He looked around the tossing ocean and observed nothing but apathetic seawater, shifting and throwing itself in such a huge accumulation that you'd have thought every river ran to this very spot solely for the purpose of watching them die.

He gripped the oars like a spear before battle.

The storm hit them like a hammer. Seconds before the boat was nearly flipped over Joshua, saw the wall of rain and wind race over the surface of the water like some phantom army, and when it hit it was like being run through. The small wooden boat rose and felt as if it stood on the aft section like a dog trying to stand on two legs, before it came crashing back down on the ocean at an angle that didn't quite send enough water into the boat to sink them immediately, but certainly enough for them to shift their focus from rowing to bailing.

As soon as Joshua pulled the large wooden bucket out from under his seat, filled it, lifted it, and poured its contents over the edge, he knew that there would be no rowing after this, at least for the time being. As he awkwardly hoisted the heavy bucket over the side his entire body screamed in protest from the steady wear and tear it had endured all day. He did it again, and this time he thought he could feel a muscle give in his side. Absentmindedly he acknowledged that his broken ribs no longer hurt, and for that he felt the slightest urge to feel thankful, but instead felt like a cowering body receiving blow after blow from a faceless group of assailants that wanted nothing more than to see him suffer, and to be thankful for healed ribs would be to feel thankful that someone had taken their boot from his neck, only to kick him in the gut.

Gerald yelled something from up-front.

"What?!"

"I said, 'we're sinking!'"

Boom. Another kick.

Joshua wouldn't go down that easily though. He wasn't quite sure what had changed from when he had been drowning in the river before; he still felt defeated, would likely die at the hands of his companion if not the storm, and for all of that, might not even die at all. Perhaps if he managed to stop caring completely, to banish his fears and accept his life as a murderer born to pay the price, he could walk on water like some messiah—perhaps he could transcend the rules of this world and hover over it with total power over its occupants only to be ultimately powerless to escape. He would be doomed to power. One of those lucky, hardworking businessmen that sacrificed everything to reach the top and when they had finally achieved all of their dreams and acquired their money and houses and wives they looked around and realized that it is nothing, and they are nothing, and that there is truly nothing left to do but die without hope and goodness, for those are the only things and to start trying now would be to forfeit everything, and to do that, they would have to be different. They would have to change who they were on a fundamental level. So they don't and instead of swallowing their pride they swallow a bullet, their achievements left to vultures who only feed upon the dead, caring not if they're buried or still walking.

Joshua fell like a limp rag doll into the ocean, and was swallowed.

He felt like he was dreaming the same dream. As if he had never woken but had instead seen a brief glimpse of the future to come and remained in the embrace of the grey-haired man with a look of concern in his eyes. Wet hair swaying. Like trees.

Joshua drifted back into the dream. Sunk down into it like a hot bath of pure sunlight. Birds sang. The engine rumbled as they drove slowly down the road. The water was dark now, and sticky, and when some slipped between Joshua's lips it tasted like copper.

A boot landed in his gut. And another. And another. Then he was hacking, his mouth tasting of salt. Of the sea. He spat.

"Hey! You okay over there?"

The voice sounded concerned, and it bounced around in his head trying to find purchase on a memory. Had he heard it before? Yes, The Harbor. It was the man who had saved him. But no...he had heard it before that. Something familiar.

It played on fast-forward. "We're just looking for the Fletcher place. You know it?" a voice asked. And then it was choking on its own blood.

"Hey! You alive? Hey! Joshua!" Gerald was yelling to him from some hunk of wood that bobbed up and down on the waves.

Joshua's mind and vision slowly returned to him and he realized that not only could he see a man that should have been dead— should have been dead at least twice over—but that he could see him by something he hadn't experienced in some time: pure, brilliant sunshine. It poured over them like golden rain from an impossible baby-blue sky. A few white and wispy clouds floated along like gentle sheep in a mild pasture. If dying is what it took to see sunshine again, Joshua decided that he'd die every day of his life.

"Joshua!" Gerald was still calling to him, but his voice was rougher and far more hoarse than usual, and Joshua figured that he had been yelling for some time.

Speaking of which...

"What time is it," were the first words to crawl out of Joshua's mouth. He rubbed his eyes and then fixed them on Gerald. Gerald stared blankly, looked around, and then gave an incredulous shrug.

"How the *fuck* should I know? Do I look like I'm wearing a goddam watch?"

"What happened?" Joshua asked, even though he remembered. He had to hear it from someone else's mouth.

"Storm," Gerald said simply. "Smashed the boat. You fell overboard. I thought you were gone for good, especially after that huge wave."

Joshua tried to remember a wave, but couldn't. He only remembered the immense feeling of hopelessness he had felt right before he had blacked out.

"A couple pieces of the boat survived. I was clinging to one of them. Thought I was holding onto an oar but it turns out I was just holding onto the ripped sail and the pole it was attached to. Lucky for you too. I was just being thrown around blindly in the dark and all of a sudden I feel something crash into me. Low and behold: it's another piece of the boat, with you on top of it. If I didn't believe in miracles before I sure as shit do now. You got away from me a bit. But I was on the lookout, and then the next time the wind threw you into me—or me into you, not quite certain which was which—I had the sail ready and tied it to that jagged piece of wood sticking out over there. Got a mighty fine splinter doing it too might I add." Gerald held up his hand to reveal a big piece of wood that had been rammed up into the flesh of his hand. "Been trying to get it out for a while now. It was probably two inches deeper about an hour ago. I'd rip it out but it just hurts so damn much."

Joshua wasn't quite sure what to say to that, so he said nothing.

All of a sudden something bumped the bottom of the piece of wood he was laying on. He might have thought it was just a wave, but then he felt it again: definitely solid, definitely moving underneath him. Joshua erupted upwards, almost spilling himself out of the boat, or at least the piece of wood he was on from the side of the boat. It contained a small piece of the floor and was joined to the back in an "L" shape. He rose hesitantly, trying not to tip and fall out.

It was hard to see at first. Just water, like usual. But then he saw something move off to his left just below the surface. Some shape or shade of dark. Then another about ten feet away. Then another and another. All around him he could see little shapes of different sizes and colors moving in one direction. Then they all moved a hair to the right, then back to the left, just a bit

And then it dawned on him, and he felt a little woozy.

They were all moving at once. Not like fish in a school or birds in a flock, with the almost imperceptible delay of reaction as the leader moves and the others follow, but perfectly at once. Joshua realized that he wasn't looking at a bunch of different little shapes underneath him.

He was looking at one big shape.

Something huge was swimming by underneath their little makeshift rafts. Bigger than any whale Joshua had ever heard of. The water was clear and it was near the surface, so Joshua could take in more and more of the creature as he focused and looked further out.

He looked at Gerald and saw that he had seen it too. The old man looked around and then stared at Joshua.

Joshua looked back down, and all at once, the creature disappeared deeper into the water. And a few hundred meters away a big ripple appeared and sent a few rocking waves over to jostle the two men around like play-things before the water settled back down and all signs of the creature were gone. He had seen his whale.

"That must have been its fin or tail or something," Gerald said, gesturing over towards where the waves had come from, a look of pure wonder in his eyes.

"Yeah," Joshua said, and couldn't manage any more words. He leaned back a little in his raft. This ocean must be *huge*. And *deep*. *Extremely* deep if it could hold something like that. Between the wolves and storms, and the odd passing of time, Joshua had always known that he wasn't exactly where he had originally thought. Not home at least. But now he felt almost totally *alien*. It really began to sink in that he was truly someplace fantastical, even if its horrors outnumbered its wonders. He laid his head back and looked up at the sky.

"You saved me," Joshua said after a while. "Twice." Joshua kept thinking about the man he had killed so long ago. And then he thought about the look on the old man with the cane's face as he had shot him in the chest.

"Do you forgive me?" The words were quiet, and after a second, Joshua turned to Gerald to see if he had heard them.

Gerald had tears running down the deep lines in his face. He said nothing.

"I'm sorry," Joshua said. "I'm sorry for everything. I'm sorry you have to be here. I'm sorry for what I did. I'm sorry for-"

The words were drowned out by a dull roar, and when Joshua turned to see the wave it was already bearing down upon them. And when it fell, it fell like the sun from the sky.

Ovin was crying.

"Shush shush shush!" Joshua ran to grab him. To shake him. To make him understand but when he touched him he left huge bloody handprints on his shirt.

They had been driving up to the cabin just for the afternoon. Just a few hours to lay back and relax and maybe let Ovin run around the yard trying to catch insects with his little net. He had found it washed up on the beach from some other house further up the shore, and when Joshua told him that the little pink net was a girl's net, the young boy had said, "but *I* have it. So it's not a girl's, it's mine." And that was all there was to it.

He would jump and stalk around the yard with the little, pink net; catching big, blue dragonflies in the morning and fat, mean horse flies in the afternoon. He would wait in one place, crouched behind a bush of lilacs that Julia had planted a few years back, waiting for any bug that dared land on the purple flowers that jutted out. Or he would race around, pumping his little legs as fast as he could trying to outrun bees and flies and small swarms of tiny gnats.

The boy was a hunter.

They had come up for a simple and relaxing afternoon, but as they drove down the gravel road, the red station wagon had continued to follow them. And as every road that they could have turned down passed by, Joshua's hands gripped the steering wheel tighter and tighter. His heart hammered in his chest. Who were these people? He didn't know them. What could they possibly want? If it were car troubles they wouldn't be stranding themselves further and further out here. If it were some sort of DNR official or state officer they would have looked more official. From what Joshua could tell, it was a gruff-looking heavy-set man in the driver's seat, with a portly, younger man in the passenger seat that could have been his son. Both of them were big, however, and if push came to shove, there would be no winning in a fistfight.

What if something happened? Why did he have to bring Ovin out here today? Why couldn't he have left him with Julia? Julia. It would break her if anything happened to them. All of those years of shared memory and devotion just gone in the blink of an eye. Maybe she wouldn't even know they were dead. Maybe they would kill them and bury them somewhere and all she would be left with would be questions. That would be terrible. Gut-wrenching. Life-wrecking for his wife. Joshua simply was not going to let that happen. He would defend his life and his son's life, and there was nothing else. No other possible outcome. Anything else was as insane as a giraffe walking on the moon or the stars being made out of iridescent gummy bears. Anything else simply could not be.

And before he knew it, Joshua was pulling into the cabin driveway, the sun blazing overhead like a galactic security camera. The red station wagon pulled up behind them and blocked their exit.

"Ovin. Look at me, Ovin?" The young boy looked up into his father's eyes with puzzlement. "You stay right here okay, but if you see daddy fall. If you hear any loud bangs or anything, I want you to jump out of the car and run as fast as you can, got it?"

The boy nodded hesitantly.

"You run into the woods and you don't stop until you find a house and you walk right through the door and tell whoever's inside that there are two men after you and that they need to call 911, OK?"

Ovin nodded again, this time a little more sure of himself.

The rest took place like a dream.

He stepped out of the truck, closed the door—*hard*—and walked over to the car that still rumbled gently in the driveway, its nose facing slightly into the woods so as to block any exit or entrance. The man inside was old, but not thin or weak looking. On the contrary, he looked thick and mean. The person in the seat next to him was clean-shaven with a pudgy face, and when Joshua stooped to look in through the window, he slammed his hands down on the door frame and watched the passenger jump.

"Can I help you," Joshua asked.

"We're just looking for the Fletcher place. You know it?" The man asked in a neutral tone, all the while his eyes flicked over the place, searching, weighing, assessing.

Joshua had planned on talking it out with them, or at least waiting for them to exhaust their cache of lies, but when he saw the old man looking around, thought about him laying his eyes on Ovin, he lost all patience and control.

Attached to his belt was a leather sheath and inside of that leather sheath was a 6-inch hunting blade designed especially for skinning and gutting large animals. There was no anger in Joshua's face as he pulled the knife out, hiding it from sight behind the solid car door. There was no malice or fear evident, just a calm and glossy look, as he simply lifted the blade and carefully inserted it into the man's neck, like a key into a door. He saw the man's eyes widen, and he tried to scream, but the blade was there and blood began to pour down his throat and into his lungs and stomach.

Joshua withdrew the blade as the man's hands flew to his neck and tried to staunch the flow. Joshua walked around the side of the car in a daze. The door flew open with a loud creak, rocked back on its hinges, and almost hit the younger man as he tried to extricate himself from the car and situation.

Perhaps he tried to run around the car to help his companion. Perhaps he meant to attack Joshua as he had originally planned. No one would ever know, for as soon as he was close enough, Joshua brought the blade up and sank it into his gut. The man groaned and the noise sounded almost frustrated. The look in his eyes was sorrow as the blade sunk in again and again with loud sucking sounds. Eventually, the man had fallen to the ground on his back and rolled over moaning with tears in his eyes. Joshua watched with numb horror as the man tried to push himself up off of the ground with his hands but failed to realize that, caught between his right hand and the ground he was pushing off from, was a piece of his large intestine, and as he tried to push himself up another foot or so of the grey, ropey organ was pulled out. He screamed in terror when he looked down and looked around for help.

He found none.

Joshua watched as his eyes finally met his and they seemed to plead with him. Then, impossibly slow, yet irretrievably certain, he turned his head to focus on something behind. He hadn't heard the car door open, but behind him was Ovin. His eyes were wide, his breathing heavy, and when the man finally collapsed to the ground and Ovin looked up into his father's eyes, Joshua knew for certain, that they had just crossed over into something—into lives that would be defined by this moment.

Somewhere up above, carrion birds were beginning to gather.

18

SIMONE

For three days, Simone stumbled along with shackles on her wrists and chains dragging behind her. They had beaten her. Kicked her. Thrown her down to her knees in front of the man with the flushed face and red beard that looked like an inverted flame, burning everlasting.

They had used a decoy. Simone should have guessed—should have taken her time. Should have followed them like she had originally considered doing, but no. She had been overcome with wrath and it pushed her into action and the intelligent, experienced man that she hunted had deftly sidestepped her attempt on his life.

Perhaps it was for the better though. She had no line on the Pale Man, her final victim, no idea where to begin looking for him. But when she was thrown before her captor, he leaned into her face and whispered: "so you want my life do you?" His breath was like sulfur. "So you want *all* of our lives, yes? Well, how about I give you your chance. How about we take you to *him*, and see what he has to say." The man smiled and his teeth jutted out of his inflamed gums like rock formations in an ancient cave. "Would you like that?"

Simone leaned to spit in his face but once again he was a step ahead of her. He reared back and backhanded her across the mouth just as the wad of saliva left her lips and was sent crashing back into her face on the back of his hairy hand. It didn't sting as much as it felt like a hundred fire ants all biting her face at once. Her eyes watered uncontrollably and for many minutes afterward, her vision was blurred and her nose ran down into her bleeding mouth.

They bound and gagged her before she could respond, which she wouldn't have done anyway. The chains that were fastened to her wrists and ankles were pulled tight and before she knew it she was being dragged along behind the caravan of spears and ill will through the indifferent landscape of sawlike trees and busted stone.

The days were long and unending, the sky stretching infinitely around the world in an ambiguous state that hovered somewhere between daylight and darkness. The frozen metal of the shackles was a blue flame upon her bare skin and she thought she'd bleed to death from where the sharp edges dug in and sawed through her flesh. At one point she lost a boot that had been knocked off-kilter, and though she struggled to keep it on for at least two hours, it eventually came off as she stumbled down a small dip in the landscape.

From there, her foot became wet from the snow, and then eventually went numb. A day later, one of her captors noticed her missing boot and observed the foot. He poked it with a sharp knife but to no avail, and when he took the sock off the skin underneath was a dark grey with huge swaths of flesh hanging off.

Simone wretched. Nothing came up.

She had had frostbite in her left pinky finger back home during the winter, but she had never seen anything like this. The rot had set in immediately, and despite the cold, it looked like it had been accelerated by weeks. She felt nauseous, the wrath seeping out of her. Her body felt like it was dying and she didn't know why.

Simone could still lift her leg, and though she thought she could feel the rot creeping up her thigh. She plodded on, hoping she was imagining it. If the days were bad then the nights were worse. Where the days were a long and monotonous slog of pain and weariness, the nights were a cold and brutal marathon of shivering and trying to sleep. So many times she thought she was having a nightmare but, as it turned out, she was just suffering in her actual reality. She would curl up and try to go to sleep, hoping that she would be well-rested by the next day, knowing that she wouldn't be.

The foot fell off at the end of the third day.

It had gotten to the point where she had to put massive amounts of energy into throwing her leg forward just to take a step, and after having landed wrong one too many times, she felt it give with a crunch as she fell to the ground. When she got up, her foot and shin bone stayed there, her leg ending just below the knee.

Truth be told, it was the best thing that could have happened, short of some miracle. After seeing the color of the skin and the way the flesh peeled off in huge chunks, she knew it was done for. She had made her peace with it to some extent, and it had become a huge and torturous task to try and walk on it.

The caravan of people was moving pretty steadily, not like how she had seen other caravans move. These people didn't meander like others, they actually walked with purpose. Even so, a few of them came back to try and carry Simone, which was both humiliating and wonderful all at once.

They made it probably a hundred feet before they set her back down again and had to think of a better way to carry her. Not too experienced in bringing back the wounded, Simone thought to herself, and then she remembered the last time she was traveling in a caravan of people. She remembered how they hadn't been keen on holding onto stragglers either.

After foolishly trying to fasten a few spears together, Red became impatient and walked to the back of the line where Simone was sitting in the snow, frozen and famished while the others tried to find a way to carry her.

"You didn't try to run," he said.

Simone just snorted a laugh.

He grinned and reached into his coat and pulled out a big hunting knife. Some of the soldiers looked suddenly eager, but they were soon disappointed as he pulled a blanket from a pack, cut some strips off of the side, and then used them to fasten the rest of the blanket to a couple of spears, making a crude form of stretcher.

Either they picked up speed, or Simone was finally able to sleep in the stretcher as it bounced and jostled her like a ship at sea because before she knew it they were entering a camp. It looked like the camp she had killed Obsidian in, only larger.

And emptier.

As a matter of fact, she couldn't see anyone walking around. The big slave pens gaped hungrily from the ground but only a few of them contained occupants. The entire place felt eerily deserted.

"Where is everyone?" she asked as a squat man covered in bristly gray hair drug her towards one of the open pens, but he only grunted and threw her in. She stumbled and went down face-first into the snow. Ice crystals bit into her already wind-ravaged skin. She rolled over with her eyes closed, and just lay there exhausted. She should have felt scared, or angry. She should have been furious that she had been thrown into a cage, but she didn't. She just felt tired.

"The slaves are almost all gone, that's why." The voice came from the doorway. "Dead."

Simone wanted to cry. But instead, she let it soak in for a good minute before she finally opened her eyes to see if the man was still there.

He was.

Despite his extremely pale skin, he seemed to suck in the light around him, without reflecting any of it back. His hair was thick and white, and he stood with a strong and rigid posture.

"Why?" Simone asked.

"I don't know," the man said quietly, and the way he said it made him sound older than what he looked. "I didn't think it was possible..."

"Not possible?" Simone wanted to laugh. "Believe me, if you're anything like your three other friends, you can die just fine."

The Pale Man snorted. "You naive little girl. You think you've been killing us? *Ending* us? Yeah, sure, you can destroy the bodies, but the *purpose*? You can't kill that." The corners of his lips rose. "In fact, you keep us *alive*. You've broken the bodies, to be sure, but when our bodies are broken we expand in every direction looking for something to cling to. And who do we inevitably find?"

The question was so clear on Simone's face that she didn't even need to say it.

"You think you can bury yourself in snow and lay there for hours on end and live?" He laughed and the sound was so deep that Simone felt it in her stomach. "The dead don't die down here." His voice was flat now. "The people you run into in The Valley are here out of their own sheer willpower. The war—the *hatred*—that they bare upon their backs are like stones. Stones so heavy that not even death can lift them off. And whenever they act on it, that person—their *victim*—doesn't *die*." The Pale Man smiled. "They just receive another stone."

19

OVIN

The plan was simple. The fire team would hit the front of the motel, while Ovin, Russ, Peter, and the dogs would hit the back. It was hard to say whether The Pack would join in the front defense, fortify the back, make someone *else* fortify the back, or just slip out. The idea of them having some sort of security detail in general made the whole situation a little unpredictable. It didn't make sense actually, Ovin thought. Why would a kill squad need armed guards unless they were just extra guns? Then again, the other kill squads he had come across in the Middle East and Eastern Europe had been much larger than four people, which is how many people Ovin's intel indicated were present in The Pack. So if he were to guess, he would say that the security was just muscle that existed for the sole purpose of backing them up when things got hairy. The idea made sense: keep the actual hands-on stuff confined to a small number of talented killers, that way the incriminating details aren't known to everyone under the sun, and if you find yourself outgunned at any point you can always have back-up immediately at hand. Actually, when this was all over, Ovin thought that he might consider toying around with the same structure.

Just a few close people.

The thoughts were flowing freely through the back of Ovin's mind as they made their way to the motel. Russ and he had run back to camp as fast as they could and mobilized without cleaning anything up. It was go-time, and they could pick their shit up afterward. But as they weaved through the streets and Ovin's training took over: checking corners, covering, scanning doorways and windows; his mind wandered. It wasn't a lack of focus, but rather a sort of *supreme* focus. He let his thoughts come freely without using any mental energy to steer them in any direction. That was how, in Ovin's experience, you saw things you didn't normally see. Keep your mind loose and nimble, not tight and confined. If you were at the point where watching out for danger was second nature, then you could let your muscle memory and training take over while you opened your mind to the enormous amount of information it was being fed by your eyes, ears, skin, nose, and tongue. You didn't think about anything. You just let it come. And when that happened, some times the strangest things would float into Ovin's head. One time while sweeping a facility in Glasgow Ovin's unrestrained mind had begun to think about cooking. About how, maybe, that would be a good fall-back career. If he ever got tired of killing people.

Now though, Raquel kept popping into his head. No feelings. No questioning her death, her family, her life. Just her face, her single untouched eye that lay like a white island among her ruined head. She spoke to him, but not with words.

With her stare. The glistening eye that scattered him across a hundred points in time: watching his father murder two people, running away, living on the streets, hiring himself out, finding a group of villagers murdered and transformed, dog's eyes staring at him blankly, laying on the hard ground with Raquel wrapped around him like a blanket. The bar. The shotgun blast. The relieved look on the man's face as he ate the lie. The look on Russ's face when he fed him the bullet.

A series of events that had pushed him to this point. Had already pushed him *beyond* this point, for the end was already written. The paths had already crossed. And he had nothing left to do but follow it through.

They moved around the back through the door. Through the rear security, the men's bodies twitching and falling as Russ, Ovin, and Peter fired their rifles. Russ moved alongside Ovin like a shark. A bullet. His eyes as hard and hot as a desert stone.

The dogs roiled around them excitedly as they streamed down the hallway like a running river of blood. The men all carrying the dead on their shoulders. Russ's mother, his brother, Raquel, the faceless bodies of those slaughtered by their weapons and the weapons of their enemies.

And it was for this reason, that when they burst through the door of the back-corner-room and found, not a kill squad, but two young men and two young women, that nothing in their minds or hearts changed. So pressurized was their hate, so great was their momentum, that nothing could be done.

A guard lay on the burgundy motel carpet with two hands clasped around his neck, blood gurgling up and through his clenched fingers. A single hole in the wall where a stray bullet had passed through from the front and found its target, the overhead light from outside casting a thin stream of light like a pointing finger onto the four huddled on the ground.

Ovin turned to Peter, then Russ. Peter was scared and panicked, but Russ's face reflected Ovin's. Some bit of information had been skewed along the way, but these were still cartel people in a cartel town. People with a security detail.

No words were spoken. Only a pleading look from Peter. A look that begged them not to do this. But he quickly complied and made a forward motion with his hand, Ovin pulling out the video camera and switching it on.

Four pairs of wet eyes stared up and into Peter's. Into Russ's. And into Ovin's.

The dogs met them as the ground meets fallen angels.

20

SIMONE

Simone cynically anticipated the small amount of food she would inevitably receive, that tiny bit of hope that served no greater purpose than to increase her misery; so it was almost a relief when the sun finally sank in the sky and her stomach remained empty. No food. No rations. Just locked in a cage to starve. Yet now she felt freer than she ever had. There was nothing she could do. No one to hunt. No possible escape. She had heard the guards talking and knew that there was some massive group of people on their way to take the camp. They would almost definitely succeed. She was caught in a raging current too strong to resist. The cold pounded her relentlessly, and her entire body yearned for food and water. She knew that eating the snow would be as damning as drinking salt water from the ocean. It was tempting, but eventually, the energy and heat used by her body to melt the snow would be gone with nothing to replenish it, and she would slip into hypothermia. The idea should have been tempting. An easy way out. But for some reason, it wasn't. It wasn't the idea that she would die, she had no illusions about her fate here, it's that—what? She would have failed? That ship had sailed days ago. So what was it then? Simone couldn't quite put her finger on it, and instead of trying harder to nail it down, she relented immediately.

Let the current pull you along. Whatever happens, happens.

Sleep seemed elusive at first, but when she woke the next morning she couldn't remember much of the night before, so she must have nodded off quicker than she had thought. Her stomach was aching now. The little scraps of food she had eaten on the journey here were barely enough to sustain her, and now that they had dried up, her body was throwing a fit. The place where her foot should have been throbbed. She felt anxious and her hands trembled.

The morning was quiet, and for a second she thought that everyone had left—that she had been caged to die alone and empty. But eventually, she began to see the others milling about. She could have tried to call them over and beg—to offer them anything both at her disposal and not. Do whatever it takes to be free. But she didn't.

Because she was free.

The realization had come as a wordless dream without image or sound. She simply woke up and knew—knew that she was truly free. Despite the cage, despite the hunger, despite her impending death, she didn't care anymore. Sometime in the night, she had let it all go. The rage, the bitterness, the revenge. All of it. There was still a dull throb in her heart where her family had been, but nothing would bring them back now. And this place, The Valley in which their murderers had chosen to live, was so wretched that there was no better punishment. For she had seen it—seen it in the glee when the man with the red beard had caught her. Heard it when the Pale Man spoke of the others living on even though Simone had killed them.

They were slaves. Slaves of fear and malice—slaves of the cynicism that told them they would never be free of a world in which pain was the only currency and hatred the only language. They were imprisoned in cages of their own creation. They were here because they *wanted* to be here, and they wanted to be here because they saw no other option—no other reality. They could break free. It was possible. That much Simone had learned in her time here.

But only if someone showed them the way.

The sounds of gunfire and dying screams filled the air. Some-where not far off there was a battle taking place, but it hadn't yet reached the camp. Simone sat like a tree in her cage until a shadow fell over her.

"He's dead," the Pale Man said. "Or at least, they think he's dead. He just took a bullet in the chest, so now they think they've destroyed him, which is wrong of course. He lives in them now. He *is* them."

"The man with the red beard?" Simone asked.

The man nodded. "You can't blame them. It's who *they* are—who everyone is. Take you for example: you were still mad at your sister, even though she didn't force you into anything. You didn't have to drop everything and move to Alaska, but you felt caged by the social pressure. You resented her for it, all the while knowing that the final decision had been made by you and you alone. You see, you're help-less to it. And I'm about to prove it to you." He pulled out a small, black handgun.

The door to Simone's cage made a groaning sound as it was unlocked. The man observed her for a second, then slowly turned the gun around in his hand, and presented it to Simone handle-first.

It was right there: everything she had come here to do. The man with the boils was dead. The obsidian man was dead. The man with the red beard was dead. All she had to do now was take the gun and point it at his chest and pull the trigger.

"There's no way out you see," and Simone recognized a note of sadness. "I tried to leave once—tried to sail across the ocean with the men who became my brothers. But we failed. We ran out of water and when we finally broke down and drank the sea it wasn't us that spit the sea out, but the sea that spit us out."

Simone thought about that for a second. She looked up at the gun from her position on the ground. Slowly, her hand reached out and she wrapped her fingers around the sleek grip of the handgun. She took it and turned it over in her hand, the brand of the gun was stamped on the side: Sig Saur. Her hands were steady as she leveled the barrel at the man's chest. His face was grinning like some spectral jack o' lantern, his pale beard like falling snow frozen in mid-air.

Simone imagined Avi's face—imagined the faces of the girls. Then she saw the face of the young man hanging. Those faces, none of those faces, looked like the man's in front of her.

She lowered the gun.

"What? Forget how to use the safety?" The Pale Man laughed but then his smile faltered. "Well," he said finally, "if you aren't going to use it then you best give it here."

As Simone relinquished the weapon she also relinquished her fear. Her life. In that moment, she relinquished everything.

"A storm's coming," the Pale Man said. "A literal storm," he glanced up at the darkening sky, "and I guess a figurative one if you count the people that are about to bust down my gate. When they do, they won't find me here. I'll have fled, but even if they catch me it won't matter. What matters, is that before I go I'm going to place this handgun in a little box in a hideaway beneath a metal shelf in one of the bunkers over there." He pointed at a thick, stone building. "When the *literal* storm comes, you will be covered in fleece-white snow, and you will live again. Who knows? Your foot might even be better!" He laughed. "So when you wake up, you can open those doors, go down the ladder, and fish out this remarkable tool of punitive justice. You might have a hard time finding me, but then again, maybe not. So, let's speed this whole thing along."

Simone closed her eyes as the Pale Man leveled the gun at her head.

"Happy hunting," he said.

And then Simone's entire world went white.

21

JOSHUA

Joshua was broken.

When he came sputtering back to life on the edge of the ocean, he thought that he had made it. What other explanation was there? What God could possibly look down on him in his torment, relieve him of it for a brief moment, and then cast him back in as if nothing had happened—as if he hadn't made peace with the man he had murdered in another life. What thread of fate bound him to this frozen hell?

The Harbor was gone. Utterly annihilated, as if by some great and burning stone. The smoke-gutted structures sat black and bedraggled upon the icy landscape, a harsh wind from the West raking over its remains like a saw. Joshua didn't care. It didn't surprise him. What would have been surprising would be finding it still standing. It would have been like a flaw in some otherwise unblemished diamond of suffering. What purpose could it possibly serve him now that he had failed again? Died again.

And he had died. He felt it now. The slow and throbbing ache of a body that has stopped working and doesn't remember how to start back up. His heart rolled in his chest like a wild animal, his lungs burning with every breath. Even his skin felt like it could slide off at any moment.

"Fancy meeting you here, stranger." The voice was the embodiment of comedy, a burnt and smiling face greeting him jovially from beside the flame-fucked ruins of The Way Side.

"You're no stranger," Joshua said in a low voice. "I know who you are."

"Oh, is that so? Then I suppose you know who your little boatmate was too?"

Joshua nodded.

"Really? Tell me then." Drew said.

"It was the man I had killed, the young one. The one I slipped a knife into and watched die. He was older though. I don't know how, but then again I don't understand anything in this place. Not a goddam thing."

Drew stared disbelievingly for a moment. "*Really?*"

"Yes," Joshua said. "And I begged for his forgiveness, and he gave it to me."

A slow smile crept over Drew's face. "Oh, he *did*, did he?" He began to chuckle, then he was full-on laughing. He didn't quite fall to the ground but it didn't look beyond him. "Well, I guess that just goes to show..."

"What goes to show?" Joshua asked.

"That simply believing something can make it true," Drew said, and he looked up at the sky with wonder in his eyes.

"What do you mean?"

"He forgave you, even though you weren't asking for his forgiveness."

Joshua stared in confusion.

"You were asking for *mine*." And with those words Drew started laughing again. "I was the one you killed that day. Not Gerald. Me. Me and my father. We *were* going to rob you if it's any consolation. It's not to us really, at least it wasn't as I watched my mother from beyond the veil as she withered away to nothing, never knowing what became of us."

Joshua's mind was reeling.

"It was me you killed. And it was me that cut a deal with The Pack when we ran into each other when they made my face the beautiful sight it is today. I told them who you were, see? Told them who your *son* was. Apparently, they had a run-in a while back. Didn't end well for them. Granted, they were the children of a brutal drug lord, but did they deserve to get eaten alive by dogs? Maybe, maybe not."

The ground beneath Joshua's feet felt as if it were about to cave in.

"Who was the old man then?" Joshua asked. "If he's not the man I killed, then who's Gerald?"

Drew smiled even wider.

"Oh, Gerald? Only the person that The Pack was hunting. Only the man that *you* were hunting. Really, you'd think a man would recognize his own son."

Joshua vomited into the snow. It was mostly seawater, and with every convulsion more came out. A stream of salt and water that could have been tears.

"Funny how that works," Drew said. "You came down to this valley because it was the last place anyone had heard of him. He had disappeared while chasing a drug lord named, Espina—I believe you've met his children, or at least what became of them here in the land of the dead—but it turns out a few things went wrong. See, this guy Cruz, the man who hired your son to do some wet-work, well, let's just say that he didn't really give your boy Ovin all the facts. He told Ovin's superior, Trent, that they were to hunt a deadly group of killers called El Paquette, The Pack. In actuality, however, they were just hunting the drug lord's children."

"Why would he do that?" Joshua rasped, his hands shaking on his knees as he bent over.

"Well, Espina was a pretty bad man. Did a lot of bad things and commanded a bunch of bad people. Some of those bad people were apparently responsible for the death of Cruz's wife and unborn son. That's where our boy Ovin comes in. He gets hired to hunt these baddies, but there's a condition, they have to take Cruz's remaining son along."

Drew reached up and scratched the scar on the side of his face. "Yup, Cruz had this whole thing facilitated. He didn't really want to kill Espina as much as he wanted him to suffer, but it wasn't all about revenge. Cruz wanted to do something for his son, give him some closure, let him see the world that *he* saw. So he fabricated this idea of The Pack: a small but merciless kill squad that murdered for sport. Anytime Ovin or his peers would ask about a group of people coming through that looked like cartel, people would just nod and point which way. They had a security detail after all, and the security looked very, how you'd say: cartel-like."

"At one point Cruz even hired a second mercenary group to kill a bunch of villagers and sew them to dogs in some sort of massively fucked up tableau." Drew shivered. "Man, even *I'm* not that bad. It was meant to push Russ, Cruz's son, over the edge, which it did. Gave him the balls and the anger to do what needed to be done. He knew something was wrong—knew that the four people weren't cartel hitmen. But by that point, he was so blind with retribution that it didn't matter. *No one* would have gotten out of there alive."

"They also paid a bartender to shoot one of Ovin's people, Raquel. Apparently, she was the only real level-headed one that held any sway, so she had to go if the plan were to work. Couldn't let her be the voice of reason in the crucial moment. Just a matter of luck that Russ happened to watch that happen too. Icing on the cake."

"How do you know all this?" Joshua asked.

Drew spread his arms out like a bird. "The God's Eye, of course. Been there yet? It's really something, I tell ya. Though it doesn't always have the same effect on people." Drew looked up at the sky again. "The view is—well—just *breathtaking*. It's also how I know all about you—about how you can't let things go. All the way back to when that drunk driver killed your father just a few minutes after being pulled over and let off with a warning."

"How did he get here then? Ovin, why is he in the Valley?"

"*Was*, Joshua. *Was* in the Valley. He's gone now. Funny thing is, he wasn't here until *you* came looking for him. Turns out the thing with Espina's kids fucked him up pretty badly. He went off the grid after that. Cut all ties. Talked to no one. Lived like that for *decades.* When he finally came back to the world, he discovered it virtually empty. Raquel was dead. Trent had been killed-in-action down in an operation in Belize. Russ was heading up the squad now, but Ovin didn't think he could ever look at him again without thinking about what they had done together. Even his parents were gone. You were off trying to find him while Julia was dying of breast cancer."

A lump rose in Joshua's throat.

"But-" Joshua's voice felt thick. He gulped. "But I haven't *been* here for decades. I've only been here-"

"What?" Drew snapped. "You've been here what? Days, weeks, years? Doesn't matter. Time is different here, you know that. Ovin followed your trail here looking for you, just as you followed him. And around in circles we go."

"And you knew he was here all this time? And you still didn't notify The Pack until I came? Why? And *how?* You say you made a deal with them, but I can't imagine how that would work in a place like this. It's not like you have fucking cell phone coverage."

"Ah," said Drew. "Let me ask you a question? What spreads like a disease?"

"I don't know." Joshua thought about it. "Hope, I guess."

"*Wrong!*" The man before him was practically dancing. "Hope spreads a lot slower than you think. People *want* to be miserable, don't you know that by now? They want to feel like everything is shit, because if it is, then *they* have an excuse to be shit. They enter The Valley *willingly.* Granted, they don't know exactly what it is when they arrive, but that doesn't matter. They *want* to be here. No. The only hope around here is the elusive specter of death. What *I* used was better. I used the only currency these people have anymore: human interaction."

Joshua waited for him to elaborate.

"What do you think these people have to talk about around here? Death? Violence? Hunger? It gets old, and people don't want to hear about it. They *know* where they are. Plus, they're suspicious of almost anyone they come across. But coffee? In The Valley? How remarkable is that? It spreads like wildfire. It's practically gossip. 'Haven't you heard? There's coffee!' These people are *starved* for human interaction, but they also want to hold something over someone's head. Tell them something important and become the gatekeepers of information. It gives them power over others. They *love* it."

"So what?" Joshua asked. "You lit the beacon so that the hounds would come running? Why not kill Ovin first? I mean, he's the one that killed them after all."

"Yeah, yeah. And they probably would have come if I'd have told them. But I knew what they wanted—what they *really* wanted. They wanted both of you. They wanted you to burn in front of him. And then when they caught up with you the next time, it'd be him in front of you. You two would die over and over again in each other's company. Death might be meaningless here, but dying isn't. There's no rationalization you could ever conjure that would allow you to watch your son die without some sort of deep, gut-wrenching reaction. You'd be in Hell over and over and over again. Constantly dying in front of each other. That's what they really wanted, and I was going to give it to them."

"Why?"

"Why?" Drew looked thoughtful. "Because I'm a businessman, Joshua. It's who I am. I might have done it a little more *illegally* before you gutted me in that driveway, but I was one wheeling and dealing machine. I *always* got what I wanted. And to be fair, that endless cycle of suffering I described? Well, I also wanted you to go through that."

Joshua didn't know what to say, so he said nothing. It was over. He had lived. Again. And Ovin had escaped. *At least there's that,* he thought. *At least he made it out, even if he didn't know that I hadn't recognized him.* He was gone. Julia was gone. Everyone was gone.

And when Joshua finally looked up, he found the dead town around him empty. Drew had also gone.

He didn't know how long he walked. He put one foot in front of the other without sleep or rest or food. The world passed by him in a haze of black and white. Of stone and snow. The sun would rise for what seemed like days on end, and then when it hit the middle of the sky it would plunge back down so fast you could almost see it moving. Time was immeasurable. There were even moments when it felt like he was going backward—when he found himself re-treading paths he had taken in the past, as if he was going to see the old man in the cabin.

Joshua walked the path to the cabin. Entered it. Waited for him. Shot him.

Or at least it felt that way. It felt like he was doing everything over and over again. Caught in a loop. Making all the wrong moves.

He killed the people up by the cave mouth. He killed the old man in that cabin. He killed Drew and his father up in that parking lot. He even killed that drug lord's children. No, he hadn't done it directly, but hadn't the choices he had made led to it? Hadn't he let his family disintegrate? Hadn't he imprinted his son with an act of violence so horrible that he would have no other choice but to replay it over and over again until he finally started acting it out? That must have been it. Ovin had always been a hunter, but witnessing a double homicide, how could he not have internalized that? Fought with it and shaped it into something constructive? Like killing for hire.

Joshua walked on. The cycles of violence playing over and over again in his head. It took longer for The Pack to find him than he expected, but when they finally did, it was everything he anticipated and more.

"Why don't you come sit by the fire?" The man spoke with a slight Latin accent. He wore huge rags of clothing, making him look like some sort of abandoned laundry pile with a head. Joshua would have laughed if he hadn't have known who the man was, but he did. He could smell it.

The odor was something like puke, wet dog, and sulfur. He had smelled it before when he had fallen into the river the first time, and now it was so pungent that his eyes began to water.

"Got any food?" Joshua had seen the fire from almost a mile away. He thought he knew what he'd find when he got there, but he went anyway. It wasn't like he had anything to lose at this point. Might as well get it over with.

"Not yet," the man's lips twitched briefly into a smile. "My sisters will be here soon. They're bringing pork."

"Pork you say? It's been quite a while since I've seen any pigs running around."

"That's because they're all pork now."

Joshua smiled and the man smiled back. He tried to play along. He wanted to, if for no other reason than to see how exactly it played out. But he couldn't. He had no energy left for this.

"They're already here though, aren't they." Joshua's voice was quiet.

"Yes." The man continued smiling. It was surprisingly warm and gentle. "And so is the pork."

The attack came from three separate directions.

The first to reach him was the wolf on his left. It knocked him down into the snow and grabbed his leg with a massive clawed hand. To Joshua's astonishment, it had opposable thumbs on its forepaws. He had just assumed that they transformed almost totally into wolves, but apparently not. Just another part of The Valley that was beyond his comprehension.

Joshua thrashed as hard as he could, but couldn't get free. He had known what he was walking into, sure, but he hadn't truly acknowledged the level of violence he was about to be a part of. The reality of the situation was way more horrifying. Drew had been right when he had talked about being unable to rationalize certain things away, even if you knew you were going to rise from the dead some indeterminable amount of time later. There was a gut reaction, and it was all-encompassing.

The second wolf came from the right, and this time Joshua got a proper look at the thing. It skulked into view in huge and lumbering steps like some sort of walking tree of death. Its arms hung down like branches with thick and obsidian claws clacking at the end of them. The creature's mouth was open and a dull, red glow illuminated an uneven set of teeth like huge, crooked nails. But it was the thing's eyes that were truly terrifying. They hummed there with an undefinable energy. Two hot coals burning like a pair of alien suns. A drop of molten saliva dripped from between the creature's teeth and sizzled through the snow below it.

"Arrgggh," Joshua screamed as it lunged forward and grabbed his arm. The thing's entire mouth felt like an oven, and Joshua twisted and struggled to get his arm free, but to no avail. He watched in horror as his sleeves burned away to reveal fresh blisters beneath.

Joshua never saw the third wolf, but he felt it sink a set of claws into his back and lift him up and into the air like so many meat hooks. The muscles in his back writhed and spasmed involuntarily as blood ran down in a network of red rivers.

"Do you understand why you are in this position?" asked the man as he stood up slowly. His smile was gone now and had instead been replaced by a look of deep sorrow.

Joshua tried to reply, but all he could manage was a garbled name.

"Ovin." The man rolled the word in his mouth. "Yes, I believe that was right. That is, if The God's Eye can be believed." The man put his hands together and cracked his knuckles. "Is a strange place, The God's Eye. It is probably what made us this way. You can see everything from up there, and I mean *everything*. I saw Ovin's entire history. I saw your history. I even saw the police man's history who let your father's killer go. Up there you can see the entire line of bad events that snowball into absolute mayhem. They weave in and out of each other like tributaries heading towards an ocean. Have you seen the ocean, Joshua? Have you looked down into it and observed that it has no bottom?"

Joshua thought of how to answer, then the set of claws in his back flexed and he jumped and howled in pain. "Yes, yes," he whimpered. "I've seen the ocean."

"Did you drink it?"

"What?" Joshua was confused for a moment. Delirium had begun descending on him like a thick cloud.

"The ocean, did you drink it?"

Joshua shook his head.

"A pity. You could have become something else if you had. Something more. You could have even been the new figure of death if you had wanted. Shame."

"I'm sorry," he stammered as snot ran out of his nose.

"What?"

Joshua repeated himself, though he was sure that it was even less intelligible this time.

The man seemed to think about that for a moment.

"Why?" he finally asked, skepticism dripping from his voice. "Explain why you are...*sorry*."

"I built this whole thing. I created this hell when I killed those two men. I built it with my own hands. I stoked the flames with my paranoia and drove my son from our house. I ripped our family apart and failed as a father, as a husband. I've failed as a man. A *human*." The words were pouring out now. "It feels like everything I've ever done has been *wrong*. It feels like I've only made bad decisions and they've all mounted into this. They've stacked up and built this tower of pain and shit and misery. And now it's all come crashing down. It's all—It's all—"

But Joshua had nothing left in him. His words had turned to sobs and now he was weeping harder than he ever had before. He wept over Julia and their broken marriage. He wept for Ovin and his shattered life. He wept for that beautiful family that could have been something great and beautiful but had instead been strangled into something feeble and toxic. And then he wept for all of the others it had swept up in its wake.

"Do you weep for me too, old man?" The voice was gentle. The man standing before Joshua was slowly taking his clothes off, the ratty layers of cloth dropping to the ground. "I want to show you something."

Joshua watched through bleary eyes as the man undressed. It was slow and deliberate and reminded him of how Julia would undress after a long day of work. She'd take her pieces of clothing off one at a time and fold them into a neat pile. A slow and powerful exorcism of the day's demons.

Finally, the man stood naked before him, his body steaming in the cold air.

"Do you see?" The man asked. "Do you see what you are sorry for?"

Joshua did see. All over the man's chest and legs and shoulders and arms were deep gashes and puncture wounds. Teeth marks, Joshua realized. There were multiple places where flesh had been bitten or torn by dogs. Some were small and shallow while others were deep and tearing, long lines of rippling scar tissue like a mountain range of accumulated sins.

"I don't have to be this though," said the man. " I can become something else. I can get rid of these scars. I can ignore them once I set my sights on a goal. An objective. I can become something greater. See?"

And at that, Joshua watched the skin on the man's face droop, the sockets stretching down beneath his eyes. If he had been steaming in the cold air before, then he was practically smoking now. An odor of burned flesh and hair filled the air as the man's skin continued to stretch and slide off in great, wet hunks. They fell into the snow in a hiss of boiling water and in mere moments the man was standing there red and raw before him, his bare muscles rippling like an infestation of writhing worms. Then, in a single lurching movement, the figure grew in size. The sound was like nothing Joshua had ever heard before. It was something between the sound of tearing flesh and rushing water.

The wolf grew again in two more big, lurching movements. Its fingers elongated with loud cracks as its legs buckled backward. Big ears snapped up on the side of its head as long, black hairs slithered out into a thick matte of black fur. Soon it was standing there in its full glory. Grotesque and hulking, a shivering mass of fur and tooth and fire.

Joshua thought about Ovin as the wolf opened its mouth, its massive canines hanging there like devilish swords. He thought about the way he had looked on the raft. He thought about the moment of peace they had shared, even though Joshua hadn't known him. Maybe that was enough. Maybe that was enough to make everything worth it. A small fleck of redemption in a sea of shit.

The wolf to the left grunted and there was a wet, snapping sound as Joshua's leg was dislocated and then ripped off. The wolf behind him sunk another hand in and then forced the back of his rib cage apart while the one to his right literally shook his arm into pieces.

The one in front though waited. It watched as Joshua's body came apart, and in the last few seconds that Joshua clung to life, it opened its mouth almost in a state of sadness, its agate eyes glowing a wondrous gold.

Fire gushed out from between the wolf's jaws, and Joshua became a burning torch in the sizzling snow.

22

THE GOD'S EYE

On the white carapace of the dead world, there lay two black dots with smoke trailing away from their centers like grey tears from sunken eyes. One of the eyes was a mere accumulation of wood that had been gathered and stacked and ignited. Not for warmth or for cooking, but as a signal. An invitation. A snare. The prey that had walked into the trap lay ripped and burned a few meters away. His skin had been utterly burned off, the torn pieces of him stacked like the wood in the fire. All that remained were his eyes. They stared wet and knowing up at the night sky as a light snow began to fall. Light and delicate winter ashes landed softly on the lidless tissue, and there it congregated until everything was blocked into blackness.

When the two eyes were completely covered in snow, the soul slept. A torn and tortured thing, gathering strength for whatever fresh torment lay ahead.

A light powdering of fresh snowflakes kicked up as the air whirled and a huge bird landed just a few feet away from the closed eyes. If Joshua would have been watching, he would have recognized it as the animal that had followed him after he had killed the man in the cabin, right before he was first pursued by The Pack. It stretched its huge and featherless wings and snapped its beak. A gust of wind blew over the fire pit and the bird began pecking at the ground. It bit and dug at the snow until it found what it was looking for.

Joshua sat atop a stone peak and observed the land beneath him. From where he sat he could see everything, not just The Valley, but the whole world. He saw every action done by every person who ever lived and the sheer amount of pain and suffering he observed would have been enough to break even the strongest of hearts.

"It's a lot to take in isn't it?"

Joshua turned around to where the bird was sitting, only it wasn't a bird now, but a man. Wren had found Joshua where he had been dismembered, burned, and buried beneath a thick layer of frost and snow. In his animal form, Wren had then gathered up Joshua's broken pieces and carried him here. The God's Eye. The peak from which one can see all of the tragedies of the world unfold all at the same time.

"Get tired of your warm house and comfy bed?" Joshua asked.

"Oh a bit," said Wren. "Not a big fan of this whole valley if I'm being honest."

The two of them sat quietly and looked out over the landscape. The wind was light for how high the peak was and the temperature was surprisingly amiable. Joshua thought that he could maybe even live up here if he wanted to. But he didn't. He wasn't sure he wanted anything anymore.

"You're not really supposed to be here, ya know?" Wren finally said. "Not supposed to look out and see all that. It's like drinking salt water. Makes you go mad."

Joshua just nodded, and after a while, he asked. "Why didn't I die? Even from up here I can't work that out."

"Alas, the peak offers sight, but not wisdom," said Wren. "Which time are you talking about?"

"I can make out most of them," said Joshua. "I was still clinging to that fear and paranoia when I went in the river the first time after being chased by The Pack. When I came out of the ocean after sailing out there with Ovin I suppose I was still holding onto a bit of that hatred I have for Drew and his father. I think I felt it rekindling even as I begged for his forgiveness. As far as the most recent one is concerned, well, I might feel more hate than I ever have. Hate for Drew. Hate for those monsters. Most of all, though, I hate myself. But up the river, when you told me about the tributary and I made it beyond the mountains, why didn't I die there? I don't understand. I had given it all up."

"What did you see when you first opened your eyes?" asked Wren.

Joshua had to think for a moment, then it dawned on him. Ovin.

"We'll follow the ones we love even through the gates of Hell. The river led you to what you were looking for, even if you didn't realize it. A shame that by the time you did it was already too late. That's the thing about time and the course of events. If our hearts are linked to our circumstances, then our salvation can come and go like the wind."

"Why didn't he tell me?" Joshua was suddenly angry. "Why didn't he tell me who he was? I would have given *everything* for him. I *have* given everything. And he didn't even trust me to believe him."

"You wouldn't have, you know," Wren said. "Believed him, I mean. He barely believed it himself. If there's one thing I know it's peoples' hearts, and you didn't even want to go with him *before* you thought he was crazy. If he would have come out and told you he was your son, well, you'd have been out of there as fast as a man chases comfort in a world of torment. Like coffee."

"Ugh," Joshua moaned. "Drew. Fuck him."

"It's a good idea, you've gotta admit," Wren said smiling. "What better signal to spread like wildfire? It reached The Pack faster than a note tied to a bird's leg."

"Yeah well, he royally fucked things up."

"Did he?" Wren shifted on the rock. "Sure, a bunch of people died in that town. But they didn't really die, did they? Even if they never show up here again, the world is full of places that people are blind to. An infinite number of Heavens and Hells that dwell in the hearts of both the dead and living. "

"I still don't get it," Joshua said hopelessly. "The dead not really dying. The water and all that. It's all a little...*intangible* I guess."

"No worries friend. The world is a complicated place. Just think of it this way: we die every day, in small ways. And it's up to us to decide what stays dead and what doesn't."

"That's awfully *New Age* of you Wren. Who are you, anyway? I think I have an idea, actually."

"New Age. That's funny," Wren said as he got to his feet. "Why don't you give it a shot? Who do you think I am? Just remember, you're about zero-for-two right now in terms of identification."

"Yeah, don't remind me." Joshua thought for a moment. "I don't know. I feel like you might be-" he felt a little childish saying the words, "-like, God or something."

Wren just smiled. "I wish."

"Zero-for-three then I guess."

"Yup." Wren moved to leave

"One more thing," Joshua said.

Wren turned back to him, his eyes questioning.

"Do you see her?" Joshua asked as he looked out upon all of existence. A gust of wind picked up and sifted his hair like a field of black and silver wheat. It was cold but he had gotten used to it.

"The girl? The one who died in the camp?"

"Yeah." Joshua said. "The Pale Man was wrong. She didn't come back."

Wren nodded. "He was wrong about a lot of things. 'Til the end that is."

Joshua winced as he remembered firing the gun into the man's chest.

"I don't get it. The grave I found down by the river, where that woman and her two kids were buried, that wasn't where they were actually buried, right?"

"We carry the dead with us," Wren said. "They follow us wherever we go, as long as we're willing to take them. You should know that by now. After all, you've got quite the cemetery in your heart. Take The Pack for instance: they're like anchors in your heart and you weren't even the one that killed them."

"But I *did* kill them. The decisions I made killed them. The Pack? Ovin wouldn't have even been there if I hadn't done what I did all those years ago. So much would have been different."

Wren looked up at the sky and exhaled. He closed his eyes and breathed in again, then walked up to the ledge where Joshua was standing. "It's a shame The God's Eye only shows you every path that has been taken, not every one that could have been. Every decision you make though will lead to dead bodies somewhere down the line. Just the way the world works. You can't take a step without crushing someone else's toes. Even the very words we speak travel the hearts of wicked men and turn into hammers somewhere down the line."

"How do you stop it?" Joshua's voice was quiet.

"You can't."

An uncomfortable moment passed. Then finally, Joshua said, "You know Wren, I'm not great at reading people, but I think that might be the first time you've straight-up lied to me."

Wren smiled. "Oh yeah? Why do you think that is?"

"I don't know," Joshua said. "It just felt wrong coming out of your mouth is all."

"Take a good hard look at it," Wren said stretching his arm out and gesturing towards The Valley in a huge sweeping motion. "It's *endless*. The pain, and hurt, and violence. From this distance, it's all there is."

And he was right, Joshua thought, at least about the distance part. But what about when you saw people up close? What about when you were so close you could see their eyes? Their faces? Joshua thought about the look on a boy's face as he hung by the neck in front of his tormentors. On the woman's face in the cage.

And on the Pale Man's face, as Joshua shot him in the chest in his own home.

.

The air swirled with the sound of beating wings as Wren departed. Despite all they had talked about, Joshua still harbored the same general feeling towards Wren as the first time they had met: uneasiness. He was agreeable and polite to be sure, but Joshua couldn't say he ever found himself to be more enlightened after one of their conversations. Only more confused.

And hopeless.

Joshua looked out at the wash of violence that soaked the world to its very roots. The crisscrossing paths that ended in pain and suffering. The whole of it was huge and unfathomable, like trying to swallow a stone the size of the world itself.

Joshua's throat constricted at the thought of it, then it convulsed as his body threatened tears. But there weren't any. The snowflakes that drifted around him like frozen tears from a Heaven encased in ice were enough. They were everything. A smoke so thick that nothing else could be seen.

It was in that moment that, for Joshua, the world ceased to spin on its axis. An infinite number of tragedies all occurring at once right before his eyes was so heavy that time itself ground to a halt. Joshua's eyes ceased to blink. His lungs ceased to breathe. His heart stopped in the downbeat of a slow contraction.

All that remained was the snow. The ash. The tiny particulates of an incinerated world that fell unceasingly to the ground like a flock of poisoned doves. Their bodies accumulating in a light dusting upon his frozen skin. Skin that was so pale and dead now, that one could have mistaken him for a statue sculpted from a solid pillar of salt.

THE END

ABOUT THE AUTHOR

Fredrick Niles lives in St. Paul, Minnesota where he writes fiction, bartends, and sells board games. In his free time he rants about movies, lurks in bookstores, and practices introversion with his wife.

Made in United States
Troutdale, OR
07/26/2023